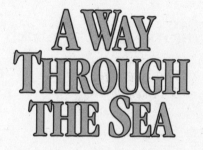

THE YOUNG UNDERGROUND

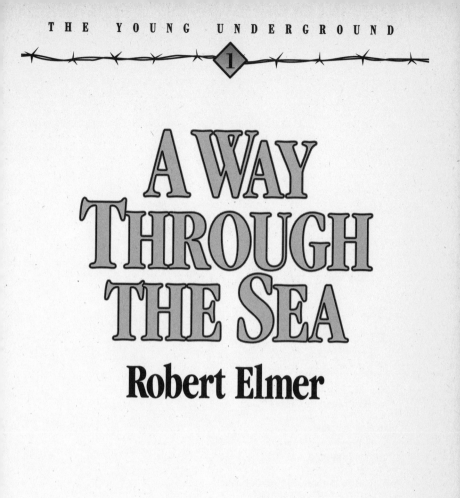

A WAY THROUGH THE SEA

Robert Elmer

BETHANY HOUSE PUBLISHERS
MINNEAPOLIS, MINNESOTA 55438

Cover illustration by Chris Ellison

Copyright © 1994
Robert Elmer
All Rights Reserved

Published by Bethany House Publishers
A Ministry of Bethany Fellowship, Inc.
11300 Hampshire Avenue South
Minneapolis, Minnesota 55438

Printed in the United States of America

Library of Congress Cataloging-in-Publication Data

CIP applied for

ISBN 1–55661–374–1   CIP

For the people of Denmark
who found courage
to stand up for what was right.

ROBERT ELMER has written and edited numerous articles for both newspapers and magazines in the Pacific Northwest. The *Young Underground* series was inspired by stories from Robert's Denmark-born parents, as well as friends who lived through the years of German occupation. He is currently a writer for the Raymond Group, a Christian advertising agency located near Seattle. He and his wife, Ronda, have three children and make their home in Poulsbo, Washington.

CONTENTS

WAR MESSAGES

AUGUST 1943

The clock was ringing right in his ear, from somewhere under the pillow. It almost felt like an electric shock, and eleven-year-old Peter Andersen jerked up, reached under the pillow, and snapped off the alarm. He sat in bed for a minute, caught his breath, and listened to make sure his parents or sister weren't making any noises. All quiet, except for his dad's soft, rattly snoring from down the hall. It had to be almost midnight, the time he had set his alarm to go off.

Crawling out of bed, Peter peeked out from behind his window shade and looked up and down the deserted cobblestone street below.

Any German patrols?

At this hour of the night, soldiers would be the only ones out on the street. They usually came in pairs, strolling along between the tall, narrow buildings, looking as if they owned the world. *Good*, he thought. *No one in sight.*

Peter looked again in the direction of the big old Church of Saint Mary, and past that, Helsingor Harbor. He couldn't see it in the darkness, and there were no lights on down in the street.

Would Henrik be awake?

As his eyes got used to the dim August moonlight, he tried to remember whose turn it was to start the message. He pulled out his silver-colored metal flashlight from underneath his bed, waited by the window, and shivered in his pajamas.

A minute went by, then two; then a faint yellow light blinked twice through a corridor of buildings. Peter scanned the street once more, making double sure no soldiers were passing below. All clear again.

After two months of practice, it had become a lot easier to pick out the little patterns of light from a flashlight three blocks away. One short blink. Two long. A long and a short. Each set of blinks, long or short, stood for a letter in Morse code, which Peter and his best friend, Henrik Melchior, had memorized over the summer.

Peter whispered out the letters as they blinked. "H.E.Y. A.R.E. Y.O.U. T.H.E.R.E."

One more check down on the street before he blinked back a reply. The strolling soldiers never seemed to look up much, but if they did, it would not be a nice surprise to have them see a blinking light in his window. After sundown, everyone was supposed to keep their windows completely dark. Peter pointed his flashlight back in the direction of the first blinking light and worked the switch back and forth, back and forth.

O.F. C.O.U.R.S.E. I.M. H.E.R.E.

Dumb question, he thought. *Have I ever been late for a signal? Not counting the time my alarm didn't go off, or the time I couldn't get the flashlight to work.* He continued blinking the light.

S.O. A.R.E. Y.O.U. R.E.A.D.Y. F.O.R. T.H.E. P.R.A.C.T.I.C.E. R.A.C.E. T.O.M.O.R.R.O.W.

Peter almost missed several of the letters, but he got the message through.

I.M. R.E.A.D.Y., Henrik flashed back. S.O. I.S. M.Y. B.I.R.D. T.O.O. B.A.D. A.B.O.U.T. Y.O.U.R.S.

Peter grinned in the dark. Typical Henrik. He was always Mr. Competition, wanting to go head to head. *So okay, we'll see whose homing pigeon wins the race tomorrow. My bird is just as fast, and he knows it.*

W.E. W.I.L.L. S.E.E. T.O.M.O.R.R.O.W. M.O.R.N.I.N.G. A.N.D. M.A.Y. T.H.E. B.E.S.T. B.I.R.D. W.I.—

There was a noise out in the hallway, as if someone had gotten up. Peter snapped the flashlight off in mid-blink, yanked down the heavy canvas shade, rolled back into bed, pulled the covers over his head, and pretended to be asleep. He heard his door squeak open, and there was no sound except his father's breathing. Peter held his breath. Then the door closed again, and the shuffling went back down the hall toward his parents' room.

That was too close, thought Peter. He would have to explain to Henrik in the morning. Peter's dad did a lot of midnight checking around the house lately, especially since the war had started. He would check the windows to make sure the shades were pulled all the way down, then he would peek outside, and Peter's mom would ask if anybody was out there, and they would worry about everything all over again.

Worry, worry. Peter thought *everyone* in the little country of Denmark was worrying these days. His parents worried about how much food they could get, and they worried about the German soldiers all over their city. They even worried about Peter's friend Henrik, whose family was Jewish. Peter overheard them talking about it once, and at first, it didn't make any sense to him. No one in Denmark had ever seemed to care about who was Jewish (there were only a few thousand in the country) and who was Lutheran. But from what Peter's father said, the Germans thought a different way about the Jews, as if the Jews were to blame for every problem in the whole world or something. The Germans didn't want anyone to know how they captured

Jews in other parts of Europe, said Mr. Andersen—whole families and everything—and how they took them to prison camps, even killed them. Peter was way too afraid to talk about anything like that with Henrik.

He did understand what he could see, though: German soldiers in the streets, German boats in the harbor, sometimes German planes in the sky. They had just raced into the country about three years ago—when Peter and his twin sister, Elise, were eight—with tanks and planes and ships, and they had completely taken over. They didn't ask or anything. Denmark was a little country, and the Danes didn't have much to fight back with. "They'll leave again after they get what they want," Mr. Andersen said one night at dinner, right after the invasion.

He did say that once, and Peter remembered it. But when he and Elise asked him more questions, their father wouldn't talk about it anymore. "We're just trying to keep things as normal as we can for you two," he said, closing the book on the subject. The way he looked at them, serious and sad, told Peter not to ask anything else.

But now that Peter and Elise had just turned eleven, the Germans were still around, and Peter wondered how much longer it would go on. The war. *They must not have gotten what they wanted yet.* He lay awake, trying to fall asleep, trying to remember anything else his dad had said. After a while, though, he gave up. Pigeon races were more fun to think about than wars.

May the best bird win, Henrik. Before long he heard his dad snoring again.

Numbers One, Two, and Three

Too excited to sleep, Peter lay in his bed, thinking back to the year before—1942—the year their birds had hatched. The first problem had been figuring out names for the ugly things. But Elise solved that on a Saturday morning when they were in their grandfather's boathouse, down by the harbor.

They had already waited twenty-one long days from the time the eggs were laid until they hatched. Then when they did, everyone was excited—but kind of disappointed, too.

"Boy, are those things ugly," said Peter, wrinkling his nose at the three squirming creatures and bending down for a closer look. "They don't even open their eyes." He didn't mention that they were fat and blubbery with splotches of fluffy down here and there, or that they were mostly blue. Elise looked closely when Maxine (the mom) left the nest to get a drink.

"Yeah," agreed Henrik, combing his jet black hair with his left hand. He wasn't blond and blue-eyed like Peter and Elise, but instead had the sharp, dark features that hinted strongly at his Jewish background. "I can see their veins and everything.

And look at those crazy crooked beaks. Are you sure they're not baby vultures?"

"Maybe they're part vulture," said Peter. "It's just too bad they can't come out cute and fuzzy, like a baby chick or something."

"Well, *you* sure weren't born cute and fuzzy," snapped Elise. She and Peter had grown up sharing a lot of things, and they were still quite close. But sometimes when they all got together with Henrik, Peter found his sister getting irritated at some of the things he said. Like now.

"So how do you know?" asked Peter, looking up at her with a grin. "Were you there or something?"

"As a matter of fact, I was," she shot back. "For about a whole half an hour before you, don't forget."

"How can I, when you remind me about it once a week?"

Peter and Elise had faces that looked much the same, with their mom's long, straight nose and their dad's steel blue eyes. And they were both kind of skinny, with knobby elbows and knees. The main difference was that she had passed him up on the height chart in the living room two years earlier, something Peter tried to forget but couldn't. He also tried to forget that technically she was older than he was.

Peter and Elise's grandfather, who was working on a piece of wood, only laughed at the conversation. "They're ugly, all right. But give them a few months. Six months. They'll be flying around, growing feathers, and turning into big, beautiful homing pigeons."

They looked over at the ugly chicks' parents, who liked to strut around in the sunlight coming in from the window. The neck feathers of the birds turned different colors in the sun— green and blue mostly. In the case of the three new birds, this would have to be like the Hans Christian Andersen story where the ugly duckling turns into a beautiful swan.

"Yeah," said Henrik. "But what are we going to call them now?"

"How about the name Thor for one of them?" suggested Peter. He had been studying myths in school, which is how he thought of the name. He picked up a broom to sweep the floor a little, waiting for somebody to react to his suggestion. Elise held the end of a board for Grandfather at the workbench, looking thoughtful.

"Nah," said Henrik. "It should fit with the other two names, like the Three Musketeers or something. And besides, that sounds too much like a Norse myth."

"It's supposed to," replied Peter. "So how about Trusty?"

"Dog's name," said Henrik, giving a thumbs-down sign.

"Checkers?"

"Uh-uh."

"Lightning?"

"Forget it."

"Tic, Tac, and Toe?"

Henrik just groaned while Elise and Grandfather kept working.

"Those are my suggestions," said Peter, shrugging. "I can't think of anything else."

No one said anything for a couple of minutes, and the only sound was Grandfather's steady sawing.

"Um . . . how about if we call them Shadrach, Meshach, and Abednego?" Henrik said finally.

Peter thought he hadn't heard that right. "Huh?" he said. "What language is that?"

"You know, from the Bible story?" Henrik looked amazed that his friend didn't know. "The one where they get thrown into a furnace, but they don't burn up? Didn't they teach you that one at your church?"

Peter's family didn't go to the Lutheran church much, except on holidays like Christmas and Easter, the same as everyone else.

Henrik seemed to know a lot more Bible stories than either Peter or Elise did.

"I must have missed that week," said Peter quickly, a little embarrassed. "Anyway, there's no way I can pronounce those names."

Henrik sighed and went back to looking out at the harbor through the little window.

"I have an idea," announced Elise. Grandfather picked up his board, and she clapped the sawdust from her hands. "Henrik's bird was born—I mean hatched—first, right?"

"Right," said Henrik, turning around. "And he's still the best-looking one."

"What do you mean?" interrupted Peter. "Yours hardly has its eyes open, and it can't hold its head up, and it looks all deformed—"

"Deformed? Yours is the one that's deformed, with all that blubber!"

Elise raised her hands, like a soccer referee. She was in the same grade as Henrik and Peter and probably smarter than both of them. They wouldn't admit it, though, at least not yet. She knew all the capitals of Europe by heart, and she often had to help Peter with his math. Her teachers at school said she was "gifted." That was okay, Peter thought, as long as she didn't get bossy about it. Mostly he and Henrik listened to her ideas. Mostly. After all, she *was* the brain of the family.

"Okay," she said. "We can hardly tell them apart just now. But since you two can't agree on a name, why don't we give them numbers?"

Henrik and Peter both looked at her as if maybe this was not one of her genius ideas. Grandfather Andersen started sawing on a new board, and Peter could tell he was listening, too.

"But they already are going to have numbers," Peter said to her. "Grandfather has the little rings ready." He was talking about three little aluminum rings his grandfather had out on the shelf, ready to slip around each bird's right leg. Grandfather had pulled the bands out of one of the drawers, the ones that were filled with bronze screws, bolts, small tools, and a whole collection of little orphaned things.

Elise still sounded sure of herself. "I know that, silly. Henrik's bird is going to be number 3341, yours is 3342, and mine is 3343. But I don't mean we should call them by their full numbers. We'll just call the first one Number One, the second one Number Two, and mine Number Three."

Henrik and Peter just looked at each other, this time without their annoyed looks.

"What do you think?" asked Grandfather, who had picked up the rings. "Do you boys have any better ideas?"

Peter shrugged. "I guess not. Sounds good to me, even if it is a little different."

"I like different names," said Henrik, looking over at Elise. "They're better than Trusty or Spot."

She smiled back, the way she did when the boys finally came around to her ideas. Not "I told you so" but more like "What took you so long to figure it out?"

So with Grandfather's help, Peter held the helpless little birds as Elise and Henrik gently pulled the toes of their tiny feet backward and slipped the rings over their legs.

"Looks too big," observed Henrik when the rings were in place.

"They'll grow faster than you think," said Grandfather.

Later, they gave Number One, Number Two, and Number Three a special feed dish all their own. Then over the next year, they worked at training them to be real homing pigeons. They kept busy with the birds every day after school and on the weekends.

It took them a while to get the birds used to going through the bars, though. Even before the little pigeons learned how to fly well, Henrik climbed up on the roof of the shed and pushed them gently through the little hole with one-way bars, one at a time, until they had figured out how to do it themselves. It was kind of like a miniature jailhouse window, except that the bars swung in from the top. After a few weeks, they started learning how to get right back to the shed, where Elise would be waiting with their favorite treat, dried peas, in her hand. Gradually, the training flights got longer and longer until the three birds knew exactly how to come back home and go right into the shed, without standing around on the roof, making messes.

Grandfather told Peter once that before the war he used to have a lot more messes, with twenty birds—all of them racing champions at one time or another. He had neatly pinned blue ribbons in a row on the wall inside his shed, proof of his stories. He had a lot of stories. But that was before—before Peter had a story of his own. Thinking back to that year, it all seemed like a long, long time ago.

THE FIRST RACE

Peter slept in a little. When he finally woke up, it wasn't to his alarm clock but to something else. Out at the entrance to the harbor, the foghorn blasted every nineteen seconds. He lay awake, counting the same way he had since he was a little boy. Seventeen, eighteen, nineteen, blast. One, two, three, four . . . crack!

He jumped out of bed, snapped up the shade, and threw open the window. Everything seemed drippy and clammy outside.

"Hey, are you trying to break the window or something?" he yelled down at Henrik.

Henrik was standing in the middle of the foggy street, with his hands on his hips and a grin on his face. He was taller than Peter, maybe as tall as Elise, and he looked like a professional soccer player as he juggled a pebble between his feet. He was always grinning like that, and when he came to wake Peter up, he usually pretended not to know anything about the pebbles he threw up at the window to get Peter's attention. Peter scratched his head, looking down at the street. *One of these days he's going to break the windowpane, and then he'll be sorry.*

"You're just sleeping the day away," Henrik shouted back. "It's late!"

Peter popped his head back inside, followed by a patch of cool fog. His alarm clock said seven. He pulled yesterday's slightly wrinkled shirt on before he leaned out again.

"What do you mean *late*?" he shouted once more. "You call seven late?"

"I don't call seven on a Saturday morning late at all," said Mr. Andersen from the hallway. "You can stop shouting out the window before you wake all the neighbors."

From the sound of it, he wasn't kidding. Peter turned around and lowered his voice. "Sorry," he said to the door.

"And now that we're all awake," added Peter's mother, "you can come for breakfast."

"But we're going to take the birds out this morning on a race." Peter opened up his door to the hallway. Both his parents were standing there, looking half asleep.

"How are you going to fly the birds, anyway, in this fog?" asked his father. He was still in his pajamas.

Peter went back over to the window again to check if there was any blue sky showing yet. There was, just a little. At least, it didn't look totally foggy.

"It'll burn off in an hour or so," Peter told his dad. "That will give us just enough time to bike out to the Marienlyst."

The Marienlyst—Mary's Resort—was the grand old hotel north of the city, the one that looked out on the Sound and Sweden. To get there, Peter and Henrik would have to ride up the coast, past the famous Kronborg Castle. It was a ride they had made several times before with Elise.

"Hmm," said Mr. Andersen, scratching his morning beard. He still wasn't fully awake. "Well, you better get something to eat before you leave. And stay away from any soldiers out there."

Peter nodded, barely paying attention. "We have to hurry, though," he said. "Henrik is waiting outside with the birds."

The boys had decided to take their two birds in the basket, let them go at the seaside resort, and see which of the birds made it back to the coop first. Elise, who was reading a big book for school over the weekend, had said she didn't want to come this time, but she would judge the finish. It would cost Peter, though.

"Okay, but what will you give me if I do it?" she had asked him the day before, when they were trying to figure out how to do the race.

"I thought you would do it out of the goodness of your little sister's heart," he said, getting on his knees.

"Maybe . . ." She crossed her arms and grinned down at him. "But if I did it, it would be out of the goodness of my *big* sister's heart."

"Whatever," said Peter, clutching her ankles and untying her shoelaces. She yanked her foot out of the way. "So how about it, sweet, lovable, tall, little sister?"

Peter ended up doing the dishes an extra day for Elise, which both of them thought was a pretty good trade.

"I still wish she would have volunteered, though," Peter mumbled to himself as he shoveled down a piece of bread with cheese and downed a glass of milk. There was a tapping on the door downstairs at the street, and he ran to his bedroom window again to tell Henrik to wait. His window was almost straight above the outside door.

"Come on, hurry up!" Henrik hissed from the street below. He had the wicker fishing basket they used for hauling the pigeons strapped to the back of his bike. One of the birds was poking its little head out of the small square hole in the top. Henrik was jumping up and down now, bouncing on his bicycle seat.

"Okay, okay, I'll be right down."

Peter hurried down the hallway to the small washroom, splashed some water in his face, then sprinted back to his room. Elise still wasn't awake. Or at least she hadn't moved yet from her bed when he peeked into her room. *Sleepyhead.* Just in case she hadn't awakened, Peter slammed his bedroom door for effect. That worked; she started to roll over and make a noise. Pulling on a pair of pants and a gray sweater that his mother had knitted, he listened for her.

"Hey, Elise, are you awake?" Peter hollered through the wall. No answer.

"Elise, wake up. You've got to be ready for the race, and we're leaving now."

He thought she must have been pretending not to hear. *She has to be awake by now.*

"Come on, Elise. I'm not going to do your dishes for you if you don't come through for the race." He poked his head into her little closet of a room. At that, she sat up, looking very sleepy.

"When are you going to let them go?" she asked, rubbing the sleep out of her eyes. Elise was usually a morning person, but not today.

"It's going to take us about an hour to get up to the Marienlyst Hotel," he said, feeling more impatient every minute. Henrik was waiting. "Maybe less if we go by the water. Henrik is outside with the birds right now."

"So what time again?" she asked.

"Okay, listen. It's quarter to seven now, so we'll let them go around eight or eight-fifteen, or as soon as it's all clear. Then it will only take Number One and Number Two a few minutes to fly back."

"What if they take longer?" she asked.

"What if they do? I don't know. Just be ready down at the boathouse to see which one makes it through the trapdoor first.

Take a clock down with you, too, and write down what time the birds make it back."

"Okay, Peter," she grumbled, "but you're making it too complicated for yourself."

"But not for your genius brain. Don't forget, I'm doing your dishes. Just be sure to get it right, okay? The second they poke their little heads into the trapdoor . . ."

"Okay, okay, Mr. General. I get the message."

Peter started for the door.

"Peter, is your friend still outside?" asked his mother. Everybody was up by then, including Elise. "You go tell Henrik to come in for something to eat, if he hasn't already had breakfast."

"But, Mom, we've got to get riding," he said, knowing he would not win the argument. Besides, she was heating up a little oatmeal on the stove, and it actually smelled pretty good. Maybe just a bite.

"Ride, nothing. You're going to get something into your stomach besides a piece of bread. Now go get Henrik."

A minute later they were all wolfing down bowls of steaming oatmeal topped with a shot of milk. There was no butter to melt over it, but oatmeal was one thing the Andersen family seemed to have plenty of. No one had ever known Henrik to turn down a meal, even though, as he said between mouthfuls, "We really ought to be going." Mrs. Andersen answered with another spoonful of oatmeal in their bowls. She didn't need to ask.

By then Peter's father had come shuffling out again, yawning and scratching his weekend stubble of beard. He was a tall man, and his sandy hair always stood straight up when he first got out of bed. He sat down at the table with the boys to his own bowl of oatmeal.

"Ouch," he cried, fanning his mouth. "That bite went down a little too quickly."

"You're as bad as the boys," scolded his wife. "Now all of you, slow down. It's not a race."

That's exactly what it was, but Peter didn't say that to his mother. Henrik was already scooting his chair out from the table, and he would be down the stairs, two at a time, in a second.

"Thanks so much for the breakfast, Mrs. Andersen." At least he sounded polite, even if he did eat and run. Peter ran after him, down to where the family's bikes were parked just inside the door at the foot of the stairs. There was a small, dark court-yard behind another door that opened to the street. The door slammed behind them, and the two boys were out on the narrow street, wheeling their way through the lifting fog. The race was finally going to happen.

The old city sat by the ocean as if it belonged there, and it had, for hundreds of years. Ancient, leaning brick buildings huddled over the tiny streets, streets that all seemed to run down to the harbor. They were paved with bumpy old cobblestones, the kind that made the boys' teeth chatter when they rode over them. But it was only three turns and a couple of blocks before they made it to the main road leading out of town, Saint Anne's Street. It was fairly easy pedaling from there, and there weren't any cars on the road—only a few trucks, four gray German army cars, and a delivery van or two. Everyone else cycled, like Henrik and Peter, mainly because regular people hadn't been allowed to use their cars since the war started.

Before they got far, though, Peter noticed the bird basket on the back of Henrik's bike starting to wiggle. It was coming loose from where he had tied it onto the rack.

"Hey, Henrik," Peter called up to him. His friend was about five bike lengths ahead and picking up speed. "The basket is coming loose, Henrik!"

But Henrik didn't hear, so Peter pedaled faster, trying to catch up. His rubber hose of a tire only flapped harder, though, and he had a terrible time just keeping up. *Dumb rubber hose. When are we going to get real tires again?*

The hoses were awful substitutes for real bicycle tires, but

Peter had gotten used to them. Ever since the war had started, and even a little before that, no one in the whole country could get new tires for anything. The German war machine seemed to gobble up everything made of rubber, so when things wore out—like the tires—Peter and his family had to make do with homemade tires. Mr. Andersen came up with the idea of sewing together the ends of a rubber hose with heavy twine and a sail-maker's needle. And it worked, kind of. Peter's Uncle Morten, a fisherman, came up with the idea to use soft, heavy rope, braided together around the tire rim. Both inventions looked pretty silly, but it was better than riding on the rims, even though no one could go as fast on the pretend tires.

Peter would have liked to go a little faster. If Henrik didn't stop real soon, or at least turn around to check on the basket, the birds were going to take a tumble.

"Henrik, hey, Henrik!" Peter shouted. But by then Henrik was out of sight around a corner and pulling away. *Sometimes I could just strangle him, if only I could catch up.*

"Where are you going so fast?" came a voice right behind Peter. Startled, he almost swerved off the street, which only made Henrik laugh and laugh.

"Hey, real funny," Peter said to him, slowing down. "Where did you come from, anyway? I was just trying to catch up to tell you that the basket was falling off."

"Really?" Henrik sounded surprised, then stopped at the curb. While he had circled around through an alleyway, the basket had loosened even more. Somehow it was still hanging on. Both boys looked in through the birds' square air hole, and the two pigeons were quietly holding on in the bottom of the basket. Peter tied the basket a little tighter, and they started down the road again.

"Only this time, Henrik, slow down, would you?"

"Sorry."

Peter wasn't sure, but Henrik sounded as if he meant it. The

old city was soon behind them as they pedaled up the coast. Off
to the right, in the distance, was the ocean. It's never far from
anywhere in Denmark. Peter could still see patches of fog here
and there, but mostly there was blue sky now, and the sun
seemed to brighten everything more each minute. Still, his
hands were numb from the cold morning air rushing past the
handlebars of his black bike. He gave them turns in his coat
jacket, which helped a little. And even though Henrik had
slowed down, Peter still had trouble keeping up. Henrik looked
back over his shoulder once in a while, checking to see that Peter
was still there.

"Can't you go any faster, old man?" called Henrik.

"Hey, show-off," Peter replied. "I've been keeping it slow so
you wouldn't burn out your Olympic muscles." He may not
have been as fast as Henrik on a bicycle, but he could keep pace
with his teasing any day.

"We're almost there," Henrik yelled back, ignoring Peter's
last remark. They were heading straight for the water now, and
on the left was the large old Marienlyst Hotel, a local landmark.
The place was known for its swimming beach, a gambling ca-
sino, and the great views of Sweden, just across the Sound. It
was a big, beautiful building, full of history, and the boys liked
to bike out here for the ride. It seemed so far away from their
home in the city, even though it wasn't really a long bike ride
away.

Henrik was waiting on the steps of the grand old hotel as
Peter pedaled up. He had taken his map out of his knapsack and
was studying it. They both could find their way around this part
of Denmark with their eyes closed, but Henrik always brought
a map along anyway.

"Here's how I figure it," he said, holding the map close to
his face. "If we let the birds go here, they'll both go straight back
to the boathouse, like this." He traced his finger across the map,

straight across the old city and over to the other side. "We'll let them both go on the count of three."

"Wait a minute," Peter interrupted. "If we do that, they'll both fly together, and they'll just keep close to each other. We won't find out which bird is faster that way."

Henrik looked up, disgusted. "Why didn't we think of that before?" he asked. "I'll bet the Brain would have known if she had been here."

"I don't know about that," said Peter. "But let's think of a way to get them far enough away from each other so they fly by themselves. It still has to be fair."

They looked around, trying to figure out a way.

"Look," said Peter, pointing to a big rock down by the beach. "If you took your bird way down there, then we could still both let them go at the same time."

"No, it'll never work," Henrik said after a minute. "They'll catch up to each other and then just fly together."

Peter knew he was right. The birds did have a way of finding each other, even when they were flying blocks away. Then a light went on in his head, and he remembered something.

"I've got it!" said Peter, pounding Henrik on the shoulder. "We'll just give one of the birds a handicap. Yeah, that's perfect!"

Henrik wrinkled his nose and squinted. That was his "I don't get it" look.

"A handicap?" he asked. "That doesn't sound like a good idea to me. You mean, like tying a rock to its legs?"

"Not a physical handicap, silly." Peter was enjoying having the good idea for once. Maybe it was because his sister wasn't along. She was usually the one who figured out all the secret plans and things like that. "All we do is let one of the pigeons fly, just like we planned. But we hold on to the other one, and then—like five minutes later—we let the other one go. Then when we get back, we just use a little math and figure out which one came back the fastest. Not too complicated at all."

Peter folded his arms, sure that he had a great idea. Actually, he remembered reading about it in a pigeon-racing book called *Pigeon Racing for a Hobby* by Victor something.

"Your sister will know?"

"Sure she will. Besides, I told her to write down the time the birds come in. I think she'll write it down for both of them." He didn't want to admit it to Henrik, but Elise was the one who had shown him the book a few months ago and explained the whole idea first.

"Oh, I get it," said Henrik. "If Number One gets back first, and then Number Two gets back in less than five minutes . . ."

"Number Two wins."

"And if it takes exactly five minutes for Number Two to get back . . ."

"It's a tie," said Peter. "But that won't happen."

"No, well, then if it takes *more* than five minutes for Number Two to show up, which it will . . ."

"Number One would win," finished Peter, "but for sure that won't happen."

"Right." Henrik scratched his chin, thinking. "Well, maybe there's another way to do it."

They both stood there for a minute, not saying anything, thinking some more. Peter was going over the five-minute part again, making sure his math was right.

"You have any better ideas?" Peter finally asked.

"No. But the only problem is, neither of us has a watch to time the birds with."

"No problem," said Peter, pointing up at the hotel. "In there."

There was a large grandfather clock behind the counter in the wood-paneled lobby, perfect for what they needed. A lot of these kinds of inns had a big clock out front. The clerk behind the counter looked at the boys with his eyebrows raised, probably wondering why two eleven-year-olds would come into his hotel to stare down the hour.

"Pigeon race," said Henrik, as if that would explain everything. He was holding the wicker basket with both birds under his arm. "Is that clock right?"

"Last time I set it," replied the man, looking at his own wristwatch to check. He was probably as old as Peter's grandfather, and even looked a lot like him, with little puffs of gray hair around his ears and a friendly expression in his eyes. "Can I help you boys with something?"

"We have to let one of the birds go at exactly eight o'clock," explained Peter. "And then the next one will go five minutes later."

"Birds?" asked the innkeeper, eyeing the basket under Henrik's arm.

Peter nodded. *Maybe he's never seen homing pigeons like ours before.*

"Oh, yeah," said Henrik. "Homing pigeons. We're racing them back home to Helsingor."

"Oh," the man nodded. "Like they used to use in the last war for sending secret messages." He looked interested enough, probably as long as they didn't let the pigeons go in his hotel. "That was before they had radios, the way we have today. Soldiers would send their messages back and forth with these birds, just the same way you're doing now. Of course," he continued his story, "for your sake, I'm glad there aren't any German soldiers nosing around the hotel this morning."

"Yeah?" Henrik asked. "Why? The birds aren't illegal, are they?"

"Illegal, no," said the man. Then he lowered his voice, as if he were telling them some kind of secret. "But those Germans are always asking questions, and whenever they start asking questions, the rest of us get into trouble. There's no use getting into trouble over something like your pets there. If you boys know what I mean."

Peter didn't know what he meant, not quite. *The birds? Illegal?*

Henrik and Peter just stood there and stared at the innkeeper. Henrik's eyes were big, as if he was thinking about what the man had just said.

"Well, come on, boys," said the man, looking down the hall at a guest. "Let's launch those birds and see what happens."

Peter looked through the lobby out the front door. Henrik put down the basket, propped the door open with a rock, and walked out carefully with Number One in his hands. A minute until eight. At the first bong of the clock, Peter waved his hand, and Henrik tossed the bird into the air. Peter and the innkeeper trotted out as Number One circled briefly over the hotel roof, around the gardens and the beach, and then headed straight back down the coast. Peter could hear his wings whistling. The bird would be home in just a few minutes.

"How much do you want to bet Number One is the first one back to the coop?" Henrik said as the three of them walked back into the empty lobby. Suddenly a green-uniformed German soldier walked up behind Henrik. He must have just come around from the other side of the building. Henrik nearly jumped out of his skin when he saw who was right behind him.

"Excuse me, please," said the grim-faced soldier. He didn't seem much older than twenty or so, blond and crew cut. He walked in as if he didn't know his way around very well, stepped past Henrik, and went right to the counter. He looked impatiently at the old man, drumming his fingers on the big walnut counter as he spoke in a mixture of broken Danish and German. Peter strained to understand the conversation, something about getting directions, or trying to find out about the best way to get to Gilleleje, a popular spot for tourists up the coast. *What's he saying?*

The old innkeeper, now behind the counter, only returned an icy stare. "Sorry," he said in Danish. "I don't think I follow what you're saying." He made no attempt to slow down to let the soldier understand better; instead, he was talking as quickly as he could. "My German is pretty rusty."

They went back and forth like that for almost a minute. The soldier frowned, waved his arms, and tried to mix in a little more Danish. The innkeeper didn't slow down for a second, doing his best to frustrate the young soldier. Any other time it would have been almost funny for Henrik and Peter to watch. This time, though, they slipped out the door into the sunshine.

"Wow," said Peter. "You almost jumped through the ceiling when he came up on you like that. I think we better get out of here."

Instead, Henrik looked straight back at his friend, and his eyebrows clamped down on his forehead. "No way!" he said. "We didn't come all this way to only let one bird go."

"But you heard the innkeeper, didn't you?" Peter looked back at the hotel and shivered. *We should be back home.* "How they used to use pigeons for sending secret messages during the last war? What if that German guy sees our bird and—"

"Don't worry about it," Henrik interrupted, wearing the same determined expression. This was not the carefree Henrik anymore. "Nothing will happen. We're just a couple of kids, remember? All you have to do is get back in there and watch for the time. When it's exactly five after eight, bend down and tie your shoe. I'll just go around the corner real quick and let Number Two go." Then he pulled Number Two out of the basket, holding the speckled gray bird firmly.

Peter felt his heart pumping double-time, but he sucked in his breath, went back into the hotel, and sat down in a soft chair. *Why don't we just go home?* The soldier was still waving his arms at the innkeeper, but the old man was sticking to his act, looking as if he couldn't understand a word. Peter peeked up from behind a magazine and checked the clock. Four minutes after. There was no time to think about how stupid he was for coming back in. As soon as the big hand hit the five he quietly padded over close to the door, bent down, and pretended to tie his shoe.

Henrik saw him from outside, nodded, and disappeared around the corner with the bird. (He was holding it behind his back by then.) Just then the soldier threw up his hands for the last time in disgust, exhaled something in pure, steely German, wheeled around, and stared straight at Peter. Peter's shoes felt as if they were glued to the floor, but the soldier just looked past him and went for the door.

It all happened in an instant, too late to warn Henrik. But the look on Peter's face told the innkeeper all he needed to know. The birds may not have been illegal, but the soldier was sure to notice. Were they for messages? Who gave permission? And what is your name? Henrik Melchior the Jew was the last person who needed to get into trouble with a German soldier.

A second later, the innkeeper was calling the soldier back.

"Wait a minute, please," he said in perfect German. "I just remembered a shortcut you might be interested in."

The soldier, who was just pushing open the door, stopped in his tracks and glanced over his shoulder in surprise. The expression on his face turned from puzzled to angry, but he wheeled around and came back in.

Peter nodded in relief to the innkeeper behind the counter and hurried out. The soldier brushed by him again, going the opposite direction. Peter didn't look up, or even breathe, until he was outside again with the door closed behind him. Number Two was still circling higher and higher overhead.

"Hey, how about that," said Henrik, smiling, as Peter rounded the corner of the building. He was back to his old self. "Right under his nose!"

"That wasn't funny, Henrik," said Peter. "You don't know how close we came to getting in big trouble." He told him how the innkeeper had kept the soldier from going out when Henrik was letting the bird go.

"Yeah, but what could he have done?" Henrik was putting

on a good show. They both knew—or guessed—what the soldier could have done.

"I don't know, but were you ready to find out?"

"Hey, I could have told Herr Corporal all about the top-secret, intelligence-gathering spy bird, right?" Henrik had one leg over his bike again, ready to go.

That's Henrik, thought Peter. *Always on the edge. Someday, that's going to get us in real, live trouble, never mind the fact that he's Jewish.*

Just having been so close to a German soldier made Peter kind of shaky. He wondered if Henrik felt like that. He had to—but then again, maybe not, the way he talked. Then Peter remembered how scared Henrik had looked, just for a second, when the innkeeper had told them his story. Henrik looked over his shoulder to see if Peter was coming, and they pedaled away.

"See that guy's motorcycle parked over there behind the building?" Henrik yelled. Peter glanced back over at the hotel. A motorcycle with a sidecar was still there under the shade of a birch tree. That was why they hadn't seen the soldier pull up to the hotel.

"I see it."

"We should have gotten some sugar from the hotel and put it in his gas tank. Wreck the engine."

"You're not serious," said Peter. "They would have thrown the old innkeeper in jail and tossed away the key. Us, too. He was a nice guy." *Here I am still shaking, and Henrik is cracking sabotage jokes.*

Peter pedaled as fast as he could. All he wanted was to get back home, away from the Marienlyst Hotel.

"Who was a nice guy? The Nazi?" Henrik teased. "Anyway, I heard that pouring varnish into a car's oil is even better. Starts right up, runs smooth, but once it cools down and the varnish dries all inside the engine, you can never start it again."

Peter didn't say anything and just kept pedaling. The ocean was on their left now, and the coastline of Sweden was clearly visible across the water. Here and there a fishing boat bobbed around in the waves; Peter thought one of the boats could have been his uncle's.

But this time they weren't sightseeing, and they didn't stop to explore any beaches, either. Both of them were pedaling fast to get back to Grandfather's boathouse. As usual, Henrik was right out in front, and Peter was puffing pretty hard, trying to keep up. Their tires were keeping time. *Ka-thunk. Ka-thunk. Ka-thunk.*

"Hey, Henrik," Peter wheezed between breaths. "Don't you think the birds are going to beat us anyway?"

Henrik looked back with his usual grin. "Number One," was all he said. It seemed as if he was barely breathing hard, even though he was pedaling fast enough to keep ahead of Peter.

"Huh?" Peter shot back. It was hard for him to get annoyed at Henrik for anything, especially when his friend started grinning and clowning. "You're crazy. Number Two is going to beat your bird by an hour!"

So they both crouched down, pedaling faster and faster as they pulled into the city. They passed the small boat harbor on the north side of the city, where the swimming pier was. That used to be a busy place, but the Germans made anyone with a pleasure boat keep it tied up, just like they made people lock up their cars. Then right on Green Garden Street, left at Saint Anne's, and past the huge steeples of the old Saint Mary's Catholic church. They were in the city now, racing as fast as they dared through the narrowing streets. The city was built way before cars came around, and the streets in some neighborhoods were almost narrow enough to hop across in one big jump. If you didn't mind the bumpy ride, they were perfect for bikes.

"Elise better be there, after all this," said Peter to no one in particular. Henrik just looked ahead and hunched over his handlebars like a professional bike racer.

They sped down Saint Anne's, straight for the inner harbor

where Grandfather's neat little boathouse perched on the waterfront. Peter seemed to get his second wind, or else Henrik slowed down, because they pulled up wheel to wheel in front of the little shed. They jumped off their bikes, let them roll against the wall by the side of the door, and burst in.

Elise was sitting on the workbench, in between cans of paint and a pile of rope boat fenders, the kind Grandfather braided together to protect the sides of boats. Her nose was in a book, and she didn't even look up. Henrik and Peter both stood there gasping, catching their breath.

"Well?" said Peter between breaths. He could tell both birds were back in the cage part of the shed. They were doing their usual thing—strutting, making pigeon sounds with the other birds.

"Well, what?" said Elise from behind the book. She was acting as if she didn't care, but Peter could see her grinning. She turned a page.

"Come on, you know. Which bird made it inside first?" replied Peter, getting impatient. *Elise always teases us like this,* he thought. *And we always play along, especially Henrik. This time, I want to find out.*

"Okay, let's see," she said slowly. "It was the one that has checkered feathers. That's Number One, right?"

"You know that's Number Two," snapped Peter.

"Or was it the one with the pretty blue bars across the back?" Elise flashed that annoying smile of hers.

"Come on, Elise, stop teasing," pleaded Henrik. Even he was getting impatient.

"You promised," added Peter. "Remember the dishes?"

"Well, it was close," she finally admitted. "But Number One was the first one through the trapdoor."

"Yeah!" whooped Henrik, pulling his fist down like a conductor with a steam whistle. "I knew Number One would live up to his name."

"Not so fast, Henrik," said Peter. "Did you forget about the handicap?" Henrik frowned. "We let Number One go first, remember? To really win, he'd have to win by more than five minutes. So how long did it take before Number Two showed up?" Peter was crossing his fingers, hoping that Elise had paid attention.

"Well, since I knew you would ask that question," said his sister, "I brought along father's pocket watch, and I have an exact clock-in time." She was drawing this out for all it was worth. Looking down at her dad's old gold watch in her hand, she pronounced the final verdict. "Number One came in the door five minutes and forty-seven seconds ahead of Number Two."

"Ha!" said Henrik. "We won by almost a minute!" Now he was really grinning.

By this time Peter had gathered his bird from the cage, and he held her between his hands. He loved the way the feathers on the bird's neck glimmered blue-green. "Oh, well," he whispered to the bird. "You did your best. It was only forty-seven seconds."

"Congratulations," he said to Henrik. "So how about a rematch tomorrow? Only next time, let's let them go at the same time, just to see what happens. At the castle."

"With Number Three," said Elise. "I'm almost finished with this book I have to read."

"You're both on," said Henrik. "Tomorrow afternoon."

4

A Visit With
Holger the Dane

Kronborg is the most famous castle in Denmark, which is something every Danish schoolkid learns before he's ten. (In Elise's case, make that age seven. She was reading big history books by then.) It's right by the ocean, and it has two tall towers, a moat, and everything else a castle is supposed to have. It was built to watch over the Sound between Denmark and Sweden, and keep track of anyone who wanted to sail through—kind of a giant tollbooth with cannons. Later, they turned it into a museum. It's right at the narrowest part of the Sound, where the big Atlantic Ocean skinnies way down before it widens out again as the Baltic Sea.

From the castle a person can see Sweden right across the water—only about two miles away. It was a great place to let the birds go, and it's where Peter, Elise, and Henrik rode their bikes the next day, Sunday afternoon.

Peter's favorite part about the Kronborg Castle was the dungeon. Down there, in a dark room as big as a cave, was a great statue of a fairy-tale character named Holger. Holger the Dane.

Holger Danske. He was huge—about the size of a truck, as tall as the ceiling—and he looked like an old Viking sitting in his easy chair, snoozing. The story went that when Denmark really needed him to defend the country, he'd wake up and come to the rescue. Peter's dad once said that old Holger's alarm clock went off April 9, 1940 (the day the Germans invaded), and he slept right through it.

Still thinking about the close call the day before, both Peter and Henrik waited an extra-long time to let a German army truck pass ahead of them on the road to the castle. And when a motorcycle roared by, both of them shaded their faces, as if they were looking down.

Elise looked puzzled. "So are we in extra trouble with the Nazis today?" she asked.

Henrik and Peter glanced nervously at each other. Even though Henrik had seemed brave the day before, Peter noticed that his friend wasn't acting like a daring Resistance fighter that day. They both fidgeted and stared at their feet. Obviously, neither of them wanted to be the first to say anything—not to Elise.

"We just came kind of close to a German soldier yesterday," Peter said finally. "I didn't really want to run in to the same guy again."

"Who?" asked Elise, her eyes sparking with curiosity.

"Just some soldier who came into the hotel while we were letting the pigeons go," explained Henrik.

"You were letting the birds go in a hotel?"

"No, no," said Peter, and he told her what had happened at the Marienlyst.

When Peter finished, Elise let out a low whistle. "I can't believe you let the second one go after all that," she said.

Henrik just grinned, looking more the way he did the afternoon before. "Well," he said, "we couldn't let one German soldier spoil our race."

By that time the three were at Kronborg Castle, and they

stood on the wide stone bridge leading over the moat. Peter glanced around nervously. *What if they see us again?* he thought.

"I don't see anyone," announced Henrik, leaning his bike against the railing and undoing the bird basket.

"Just to be safe," said Elise, "let's forget about your handicaps."

"Or about anything fancy, like letting the birds go five minutes apart," added Peter. In his mind he could still see the soldier staring at him for that brief moment the day before.

Henrik was balancing now on the low wall of the bridge leading across the moat to the castle.

"As you wish, my dear fellow pigeon trainers," he said to them, starting to get silly. He did a low stage bow from the top of the wall to his only audience. Since the war had started, there weren't any tourists around. But the Germans had insisted that since everything was "normal," this castle would remain open as usual.

"O Romeo, Romeo, wherefore art thou Romeo?" Now Henrik was really getting into it.

"Wrong play, Henrik," Elise corrected him. "This is Hamlet's castle, remember? Not Romeo and Juliet."

"Oh, yeah. Well, at least I got the Shakespeare part right."

He did get the Shakespeare part right. Shakespeare wasn't Danish, but he wrote about Hamlet, the Prince of Denmark, in one of his famous plays. The castle was his home and the setting for the play. Mr. Isaksen, the boys' teacher, told them they would read the play probably next year.

"So what are we going to write on the bird's note?" asked Henrik, hopping down. The note was going to Grandfather; Elise had talked him into checking on the birds. They might come in at about the same time, but one of them was bound to win. And Peter had already clipped a little metal capsule on Number Two's tiny leg, the kind of message holder that screwed apart. It was just big enough to fit a little note inside. Mr. Andersen had ordered it from Copenhagen, from a place that made pet supplies, leashes and collars, cages, bird stuff.

"I have an idea," said Peter. "How about let's write 'Help. Locked in the castle with Holger the Dane. Can't find Hamlet. Can't wake him up. Henrik, Peter, and Elise.' "

"That doesn't make sense," said Elise. "Where's Hamlet supposed to be?"

"Just a joke, Elise," said Peter.

"Well, scratch the part about Hamlet, and it will make more sense," suggested Henrik.

"Okay, okay," agreed Peter. He thought Henrik was always agreeing with his sister. But he pulled a pencil stub from his pocket and started writing the message on a scrap of paper. Elise held Number Two, who squirmed a little, while Henrik checked the little strap around the bird's leg to make sure it was on tight. All set.

Next Henrik carefully pulled his own bird out of the wicker basket, stroking him softly as he did. These birds were getting a workout lately. Elise pulled out Number Three, who was thrashing around a little more than the other two.

"Ready?" asked Peter as they looked over each bird. No feathers missing or anything. "On the count of three. One, two, three!"

This was the part Peter liked the best, when the birds flew out of their hands, and he could hear their wings clapping and whistling as they flew a few happy circles above. The three birds weaved in and out of the castle's towers, over the water for a moment, then straight back to their home just across town.

"I still can't figure out how they always know the way," said Henrik as he looked off in the direction the birds had taken.

"A book I was reading said they have some kind of built-in compass," said Elise. "Plus they can tell where they're going by the way the sun is."

"Hmm . . . the sun," said Henrik. "You're always reading something, aren't you?"

"Yeah, well, let's go see who won this race," said Peter. He wasn't sure about internal compasses; he was just eager for the rematch. Maybe Number Two would make it home first this time.

"What's your hurry?" asked Henrik. "Let's not rush today. It's still early, and it's Sunday, right?"

So the three of them pedaled the long way around—the same way Henrik and Peter had gone the day before, only in the opposite direction. Elise wasn't quite as fast a pedaler, but she kept up pretty well. Peter saw the ocean through the trees for a moment as they made their way along the shore road. They hadn't gone more than five minutes, though, when Elise slammed on her brakes. Her tires squirmed and complained, and she nearly lost her balance.

"Hey, wait, you guys," she yelled. "I saw something!"

Henrik and Peter circled around, and they all took a closer look at what appeared to be a bicycle tire hidden in the bushes. It was a tire, all right, attached to the rest of a bike. Uncle Morten's bike.

"Are you sure it's your uncle's?" asked Henrik.

"Positive." Peter pointed to the little light on the front fender. "He keeps it in the boathouse. I'd know it anywhere. But I don't know why he would ride it out here."

"Maybe it's stolen," Elise suggested. "Maybe the thief stashed it here in these bushes, and he's coming back for it."

Henrik found a rough path that led from the side of the road and into the woods. It started right at the bush where the bike had been stashed. Peter looked at Elise, who kind of shrugged her shoulders. Without saying anything more, they pushed the bike back into the bush, parked their own bikes behind another bush, and started down the path.

The three of them had explored this area before, but Peter

couldn't remember exactly if this trail led straight to the beach or if it just wandered through the woods.

"What do we do if we find a thief in the woods?" Peter was in the lead and turned to whisper to Henrik behind him. They almost collided.

"Here, let me go first," said Henrik as he stepped past Peter. Henrik was usually the first one at school to stand up to bullies, or score a goal in soccer, or climb to the top of the school building to fetch a lost ball. He was also the first one in the neighborhood to break his leg falling out of a tree, and he got into more of that kind of trouble than anyone, mostly from all the crazy ideas he came up with. Not smart-aleck trouble, just getting-into-things trouble.

Peter? He was the one who could get the pigeons to perch on his shoulder and eat out of his hand, the one with the stamp collection, the one who liked to draw pictures of airplanes. Maybe he wasn't as smart as his twin sister, but he was the one who usually figured how to get out of the trouble they got into, like the time they were going to raise and sell hamsters. (He shuddered every time he thought about that one.)

Mostly, Peter didn't mind being in the middle. The way he looked at it, he, Henrik, and Elise were all just good at different things. Elise was reading long chapter books when she was only six years old, and she could cook practically anything their mom could. The year before she had won a prize at the school science fair for her experiment with plants, and she was the best piano player in the school. But between the three of them, there was no doubt: Henrik was definitely best at leading the way on a trail like this.

The path twisted down through a dense stand of trees and bushes, and the branches whipped at their arms and legs as they passed through. Overhead, silvery beech trees formed a canopy, and the sun only broke through in splinters. If Peter hadn't been so worried about running into a thief in the woods, he would have enjoyed it.

Suddenly Henrik froze and signaled with his hand to the others. Peter could see nothing but heard voices up ahead. Two voices. One of them was Uncle Morten's, but he wasn't speaking in Danish.

"It's just my uncle," Peter whispered into Henrik's ear. "No thief." So they tiptoed around a bend in the trail and stood awkwardly at the edge of a clearing.

The Swedish man standing next to Uncle Morten was short and dressed like a fisherman in boots and gray work clothes. Uncle Morten towered over him, light haired like Peter and Elise, but large, well built, and bearded. He stopped what he was saying in midsentence, looked up, and stuffed an envelope into his shirt.

"Hi, Uncle Morten." Peter tried to sound casual. "We saw your bike in the bushes by the side of the road, and we weren't sure. We just came in to see if there was a thief in here or anything."

"Oh, hi, kids." Uncle Morten took a breath, looking normal again. The fisherman still didn't look so sure. "You kind of caught me off guard there for a minute." Then he saw that they were staring at the other man. "Olaf, this is my nephew Peter, my niece Elise, and their friend Henrik. They're fine."

Peter thought that was a strange thing to say. *What else—are we supposed to be sick or something?* But before he could wonder anymore, the Swede was gone. Peter didn't know if his uncle knew they had heard him talking in Swedish with the other man.

"Here, I have to go back to town," said Uncle Morten. "Is that the way you kids were going?" He was doing his best to sound cheery, but he looked embarrassed about the other man. Peter wasn't sure why. "I'll ride back with you—that is, if my bike is still there." Henrik hadn't said a word, and Elise was quiet, too.

Uncle Morten led the way back up the trail toward the road and their bikes. Peter was still wondering who this Olaf was when Henrik held him back for a second, grabbing his arm.

"I saw something else," he whispered hoarsely into Peter's ear.

Peter just looked at him with his "What next?" expression.

"Right as we were coming up the path, I saw your uncle giving that Swedish guy a lot of money. A *lot* of money! The guy was counting it when we walked up."

Elise, who was following Uncle Morten at a distance, turned around and frowned at Peter and Henrik. She made a "Be quiet!" sign with her finger on her lips.

Whatever it all meant, Uncle Morten never volunteered any explanations, at least not for a while. No one said much on the ride back to the boathouse—maybe because they were wondering about the mysterious Swede—and Uncle Morten seemed content to stare straight ahead as he rode. In fact, no one said a word until they pulled up to the door of the little shack. No one seemed in a hurry, either, and they carefully leaned their bikes against the outside wall by the door.

When they peeked inside, Grandfather told them Number Three had won that time, which made Elise grin real big. That must have been all she wanted to know because without a word she turned around, took her bike by the handlebars, and started off. For once not wanting to stay around the boathouse, Henrik and Peter followed her.

"Bye, Uncle Morten. Bye, Grandpa," called Peter.

"See you later, kids," came Uncle Morten's voice from inside the shed.

The three walked their bikes in silence, not knowing what else to do with the day. "Oh well," said Peter, trying to think of a joke as they headed toward home. They were tired of riding, and disappointed at the way things had turned out with Uncle

Morten. "At least Number Two came in second this time."

But what was Uncle Morten doing in the woods? Peter thought again as he pushed his bike past a pothole in the street. Henrik and Elise said nothing more.

5

THE WIND CHANGES

Peter, Elise, and Henrik spent a lot of time down at Grandfather Andersen's boathouse the rest of the summer, but when they ran into Uncle Morten, no one ever mentioned their meeting in the woods. Peter's uncle didn't act differently, though, probably because he hadn't realized how much the three had seen. Peter decided that since he couldn't really figure it out, he wouldn't think about it anymore, and he tried not to let it bother him. But Henrik brought it up again one afternoon when they were starting a paint job on a little rowboat inside the shed.

Elise had managed to find a couple old cans of paint and had poured one called "Gunmetal Gray"—mostly hard with chunks of dried paint—into a larger, older can of something called "Easter Lily Yellow." Then she skimmed off the top with a rag and carefully stirred the lumpy new blend. The boys grinned when they saw the ugly-awful color it made.

"A new discovery," Grandfather told them as he left on an errand with Elise. They had to pick up some supplies for Grandfather's fishing boat. "You should call it 'Dead Lily.'"

So Peter crawled underneath the upside-down boat with a little coffee can full of Dead Lily while Henrik painted the top. It seemed like a good idea at the time. They worked quietly for a while before Henrik said something.

"I've been thinking," he announced.

"Yeah?" replied Peter, afraid of what his friend might say. "About what?"

"About your uncle." Henrik was serious. "And I've got it figured out. He's either a big-time gambler, or a bank robber, or he's in the Resistance."

Peter thought his friend sounded as if he had just solved the perfect crime.

"Come on, Henrik," said Peter. "You know my uncle's not a crook. He and my grandfather are the only ones in the family who go to church, besides when everyone goes on Easter and Christmas."

"So what about him being in the Underground, the Resistance?"

"What does that have to do with throwing around a lot of money?"

"I don't know," said Henrik. "But you know the other guy was Swedish. We both heard them talking in the woods that day. Elise, too. Maybe it was Underground business. Payment for smuggling sabotage people over to Sweden or something."

Peter thought about it for a minute. His uncle in the Underground? That was a growing group of people who were fighting back against the Germans—blowing up factories and that sort of thing. The Underground's secret mission was to make it as hard for the German invaders as they could. One of the groups called themselves "The Helsingor Sewing Club," a cover name Peter liked. It was dangerous and serious, but they were the country's heroes, really. The only thing was, no one knew who they were, it was so secret.

"We'll have to ask the Brain what she thinks about it when she gets back," said Henrik.

"Okay, maybe, but I don't think she knows any more than we do. She hasn't talked about it."

Just then Dead Lily dripped through a crack in the boat, square onto Peter's nose, and then onto the rest of his face. Henrik didn't even notice. And because Henrik was standing right next to the boat, his legs kept Peter from rolling out of the way.

"Hey!" Peter yelled up from under the boat. "You're getting Dead Lily all over me!" He shoved Henrik's leg as hard as he could and wriggled out from under the boat like an inchworm in high gear. Henrik made a little hop to get his balance, came down sideways on his foot, and crashed right on top of Peter.

That's when the rest of the paint found them. As Henrik fell, he swept his arm wide, caught the side of the coffee can full of Dead Lily, and sent it showering all over. They lay there in a heap, dripping with yellowish gray paint.

"You look ridiculous," said Peter, getting up. He was wondering whether to laugh, cry, or throw the rest of the can at Henrik.

"Looks kind of pretty on you, Peter." Henrik was the one with the sense of humor, the one who found a joke in everything. "Matches your light hair." He made a funny face, puckering up his fish lips as he got up and looked for a rag.

"Cut it out, Henrik," sputtered Peter, by this time disgusted at the whole mess. "Your mom is going to kill you for this."

"Yeah? So's your mom," he came back. Henrik had paint splattered on his dark hair, his face, and all over his clothes.

Peter wondered how they were going to get all the paint off. He started to say something, then he giggled and it was all over. He gave up trying to be mad. The two of them couldn't stop laughing. They were still laughing when Grandfather and Elise came back.

She gasped, and Grandfather stopped before he had the door

all the way open. His big, wide shoulders almost looked as if they wouldn't fit through the doorway. Grandfather used to be a sailor, and he still seemed young like one, even with his wrinkled face.

Peter and Henrik sneaked a glance at him, waiting for him to say something. Henrik was still snorting and giggling, and Peter felt pretty silly.

"Well," Grandfather finally cleared his throat, not moving from the doorway. He pulled at his chin and tried to look mean. "I can see you two have really mastered the technique, haven't you?" He walked over to his workbench, brought out a couple of rags from a box below, and tossed them over to the boys. "There's a little bit of paint thinner in the can by the window," he said, pointing over at a shelf. "But don't use more than a cupful. You'll need it for real painting. Clean up the floor when you're done with yourselves."

Peter knew that gasoline was precious, with the German troops taking most everything the Danes had. Paint thinner being kind of like gas, it must have been stashed away from since before the war started. So Peter was surprised when Grandfather hadn't been angrier. The old man only returned to the pump he was taking apart on the workbench. He was even chuckling to himself.

Peter turned to Henrik, who was rubbing off paint with a thinner-soaked rag.

"Don't worry," said Henrik, scrubbing at a spot on his neck. "I only spilled a little can. It could have been a lot worse. And besides," he added with a smile, "you were the one who made me fall."

Peter was about to clobber him with his paintbrush when Elise came over with another rag and helped them scrub up a little more.

"I can't believe you two made such a mess," she said in her best motherly tone. Peter had seen her catch the worst dirt plenty of times. But this time, she had stayed clear of every paint speck.

"Thanks, Mom," he teased. "I needed that."

She threw the rag at him, but he ducked and it hit Henrik square in the face.

"Bull's-eye!" shouted Peter, forgetting for a minute that Grandfather was still around.

Henrik must have forgotten, too, because he whooped and pitched the rag straight back at Elise. But now Peter was in the line of fire, and it hit him on the back of the head.

"Hey, no fair," said Peter.

By then Grandfather was getting annoyed. "All right, that's enough, you kids. Clean up and get out now. Your mother wants you back soon for dinner, anyway."

"Oh, yeah," added Elise. "I forgot to tell you. We stopped at home on the way over here, and dinner's going to be ready in fifteen minutes. You two better get cleaned up in a hurry." She picked up the rag carefully between two fingers and tossed it at Peter while wrinkling her nose. "I wonder why I still hang around with two boys who throw paint at each other."

"We're just a lot of fun," replied Peter. "Your other friends are kind of boring."

"They are not!" retorted Elise. "Susan and Tina are lots of fun. See you at home." Then she turned on her heel and was out the door.

Sisters, thought Peter. *She should have been there when the real paint was flying.* Then he thought about himself and Henrik, splattered with that sickening yellow color, and he laughed to himself. Elise had, after all, mixed it up for them.

By then, the two boys were mostly cleaned up, and Henrik carefully put the top back on the can of paint thinner.

"Sorry about the mess, Grandpa," said Peter as they headed for the door. There was still a big yellow-gray spot on the wooden plank floor, where the paint had spilled.

His grandfather looked over at them with a trace of a smile

on his face. "Don't worry too much about it, boys," he said. "I'm just not sure what your mothers are going to say. They're going to think I let you do finger painting." Then he put his pretend-serious expression back on. "Now get on home to dinner. I hear there's pigeon stew cooking."

That was his regular joke, but they laughed anyway and yelled goodbye as they walked out. They went the long way around, along the water. It was warm out, and lots of people were enjoying the summer evening, strolling along the quayside in Helsingor Harbor.

Next to Grandfather's combination boathouse and pigeon coop, Peter liked the harbor best. It was a mix of fishing trawlers, small freighters, ferries that sailed right over to Sweden, tugs, and other workboats. Uncle Morten unloaded his boat there, too. Actually, the boat still belonged to Grandfather, but the two of them had been fishing together for as long as Peter could remember. They still went out together, but it was Uncle Morten more and Grandfather less. No one seemed to mind the arrangement.

Their boat, the *Anna Marie*, was named after Peter's grandmother, the one he had never met. He was hoping to see the boat come in, so he and Henrik sat on a stone bench with a good view of the harbor entrance.

"We never figured out your uncle," said Henrik, watching the boats as they came in. He was looking straight ahead, scratching a little patch of paint off his elbow.

"Nope," replied Peter. They glanced at each other for a second. Peter wondered why Henrik was trying to think about it so much, even as he himself was trying his best to forget it. "But what do we do? We can't just go up to him and say, 'Hey, Uncle, are you in the Resistance?' "

"No, I guess not," said Henrik. "I just can't stop thinking about that meeting in the woods. It's like a big mystery we've just *got* to solve."

"Remember, he's still my uncle," said Peter.

"Right. But we can keep our eyes open, and if—"

"Here he comes," Peter interrupted Henrik. He could just make out the bright, clean blue hull of the *Anna* coming through the breakwater that separated the harbor from the waves of the Sound beyond. Uncle Morten was leaning out of the little pilot-house; he spotted Peter and Henrik, and waved to them. They waved back.

Morten scuttled through the narrow opening and made for his spot at the pier, the old engine making its funny *chug-cough, chug-cough* sound. It was an ancient boat, originally built for sail. Still, it looked better than most of the newer ones, the way Morten babied it. A noisy flock of seagulls followed close behind— a good sign. They were quick to swoop down on whatever the big fisherman tossed in his wake. Peter's uncle was the only fisherman the boys knew who could navigate, steer, fish, and clean up afterward, all at the same time. When he pulled up to the pier he had his catch all packed away, ready to sell to the harbor's fish buyer, and all the scrap fish thrown overboard. Usually there was no wait, the way he did things.

"Heeey, Uncle Morten," Peter yelled, grabbing the line that was thrown to him. "Catch anything?"

"Catch anything?" Uncle Morten called back. "Don't you see the gulls?"

Peter and Henrik helped tie up the *Anna* while Morten rigged a crate of herring to the end of a cable. Since it was low tide, Peter had to crank the handle of a small crane on the top of the dock until the box of silvery fish was hauled up to dock level. His arms strained as the catch seemed to get heavier. Then Uncle Morten swung his big muscled legs up the ladder and over the top rung, and brought the crate in. "Thanks for your help," he said. "You're going to have to come out with us one of these times, as soon as my brother feels you're old enough."

His brother was Peter's dad, who hadn't given in yet to letting Peter or Elise go out with Grandfather and Uncle Morten. Henrik seemed to have cold feet about asking his own parents, and Peter wondered if they would ever say yes anyway. *One of these days.*

"Hey, speaking of your dad," said Uncle Morten, looking at his watch, "don't you two boys ever eat dinner?"

"Dinner!" Peter's heart skipped a beat. He hadn't even thought of the idea since Elise had come to get them at the boat-house. Now he would be in trouble for sure. Henrik moaned.

"I totally forgot, too," said Henrik. "We better go, Peter."

They started running back toward town before Henrik had finished the sentence. They raced down Stengade—Stone Street—past Helsingor's huge old church with the tall spires, and past the old brick City Hall. Ahead of Peter, Henrik turned one way to get to his house and waved back without looking. Peter turned the other way onto his narrow street, Axeltorv Street—Axel's Market Street. This was another one of those times when he was glad he didn't live far from the harbor.

As Peter rushed past the bakery two doors down from his apartment, the baker, Mr. Clausen, was just locking up for the night. Usually, Peter would have stopped to say hi, but he ran past as fast as he could go.

"Late again, Peter?" called Mr. Clausen, chuckling.

It had been fifteen or twenty minutes down at the harbor, at least. Peter wasn't sure, but he knew it had definitely been longer than a few minutes. *Dinner? How long did Elise say it would be? Ten minutes? Yeah, I'm going to be in trouble. Again.*

Peter pushed open the street-level door, then took the long, narrow stairway three steps at a time. Out of breath at the top, he was afraid to look over at the table, where everyone was sitting, finishing dinner. Elise gave him one of her "Where were you?" looks. Peter knew he was in deep, hot water. Their mother was the first to say anything after Peter sat down, but it took a minute.

"You heard your sister tell you dinner was ready?" Her small, pretty face—framed by her shoulder-length, curly red hair—normally wore a smile. She was a little woman, smaller even than her growing children. Mr. Andersen's pet name for her was "Spunky Owl," which doesn't translate very well from the Danish but which fit her perfectly. Tonight she was not smiling.

"Maybe I didn't say exactly how long it was to dinner," Elise piped up, obviously trying to defend her brother. Not a chance.

"I was asking Peter," said her mother, waiting for Peter's answer.

He nodded, looking down. "She said it was going to be ready soon."

"Too bad it's ice-cold now," said Mr. Andersen, his voice sounding as cold as the food on Peter's plate. "Finish it and go to your room right away. No staying up tonight."

Peter nodded again, relieved at the light punishment.

"You know this isn't the first time," his mother continued. Peter knew she would say that, too. "What were you investigating this time, a crab or a sailing ship from China?" That wasn't quite a joke, but Peter hoped it was a sign she was lightening up. Elise sat stiffly in her chair, as if waiting for the storm to pass.

"I was just helping Uncle Morten tie up the boat and bring up the fish," Peter explained in his best "I'm really sorry I forgot to come to dinner again on time" voice. He knew by the look on his parents' faces that apologies weren't going to do much good this time.

He chewed in silence—his mouth full of cold potato. The fish and cabbage were cold, too, but it didn't matter much. Since the war had begun, everyone's dinners had gotten plain and cold.

"And your mother didn't work hard on that food to have you not show up," added his father. Now Peter was getting it from both sides of the table. Maybe if it was *flaeskesteg*, the delicious

roast pork they used to have before the war, it would be easier
to remember and come to dinner on time. No, he didn't dare say
that. His mother couldn't help it if all she had to buy food with
was ration cards, and no one had enough bread, sugar, bacon,
butter, or coffee. Mrs. Andersen got the cards every two or three
months at a Ration Office; she needed them every time she went
to the store. And when they were gone, that was it.

"I'm really sorry, Dad," said Peter, finishing his glass of water. "I'll try not to forget again. Really." He looked up, and both
his parents were frowning at him. Elise, who always acted nervous when her brother got into trouble, started clearing plates. It
wasn't because Peter was trying to disobey, at least not in a stick-
ing-your-tongue-out kind of way. It was just so easy to forget
sometimes, and then when he remembered, it was too late. Only
that wasn't much of an excuse anymore, and Peter knew it. He
finished his cold meal, piled the dishes by the sink, where Elise
was doing them, and started shuffling down the hall. He sighed.

"And what's that funny color all over your hair?" his mother
asked.

"Um, nothing," he replied, closing his bedroom door behind
him. *Please, not more trouble.* "Just some Dead Lily," he said
through the door. His room was at the end of the hall, and it was
not much more than a closet, really: big enough for his bed and
a small dresser. If he stood on his bed, he could have seen the
harbor through his window—that is, if all the other buildings
weren't in the way. Elise had a room just like it, one door down.
Their parents shared a slightly larger bedroom. Though their
rooms were small, they knew they were lucky. A lot of their
friends at school didn't have their own rooms.

Even during the long summer evenings, like that night, it
never seemed to get too hot in their apartment. Mrs. Andersen
would open up the large double windows in the living room,
and the smell of her flowers floated all through the apartment.

She was especially proud of her purple flowers; Peter forgot what they were called.

He lay on top of his bed with his clothes on, smelling the late summer. Elise was still washing the last dishes in the kitchen. Outside, past the flowers, he could smell a little salt air from the Sound, a little bit of fish—maybe from his uncle's boat, maybe from his hands. Sometimes he pretended that he could even smell all the way to Sweden, that smudge of land across the water.

Peter and Elise had never been there before, but Uncle Morten had said it was full of woods and lakes, even a few mountains. Just across the Sound. Peter listened hard for anything that sounded like the ocean—the *chug-cough* of a fishing boat, or the squeal of a gull. But all he heard were voices in the next room, his parents discussing something, and then a shuffling sound coming under his door.

Elise. It has to be. He looked down and saw the note she had stuck under his door. He rolled over onto his stomach and reached for it.

"Peter, Dead Lily looks lovely on you. Just your color. P.S. I think I've figured out what Uncle Morten was doing in the woods."

She had? He wadded up the note, yanked open the door, and charged down the hall after her. Just then, Mr. Andersen stepped out into the hallway from the living room, and they nearly collided.

"Going somewhere?" he asked.

"No . . . yeah, I mean," Peter stuffed the note into his pocket. Talking with his father about Uncle Morten was one of the last things he wanted to do. "Um, I better go to the bathroom before I go to bed," he mumbled. "Clean up a little."

"It's back the other way, Peter," his dad said. "But we'll say good-night to you here. You know we love you, even when you're in trouble."

"I know, Dad," he said as he disappeared into the bathroom. "I love you, too."

As he lay in bed a few minutes later, Peter couldn't keep his mind on the history book he was reading. He kept thinking about Uncle Morten. Uncle Morten the pirate. Uncle Morten the gambler. Uncle Morten the Resistance fighter. Which one was he? Then he caught himself. *Don't think about it. It's none of your business, anyway.*

What didn't make any sense to Peter was that his Uncle Morten was supposed to be the one who was the most religious in the family, the one who sometimes talked about prayer meetings, that kind of thing. Once, a couple of years ago, Peter and Elise had even gone with him to a Thursday night meeting at a small house-church on Belvedere Way, on the edge of town. Just out of curiosity.

A soft knock interrupted his thoughts. He stuck a finger in his book and looked up.

"Peter, can I come in?" It was Elise.

"Sure." He was still curious about her note but tried not to be.

Elise cracked open the door and leaned against the side of the doorway without coming in. "So did you get my note?" she asked.

"Yeah, I got it. You're just like Henrik. Why can't you two forget about the whole thing?"

"Forget about it?" she said, her voice going above a whisper. "Are you kidding? Don't you want to know?"

"Not really," he said, opening up his book to where he left off. "I just want to read my book and not get in trouble."

"Oh, come on," she pleaded. "Listen, there's only one thing it could have been."

"We're still talking about Uncle Morten in the woods with the Swedish guy, right?"

"Of course, silly. Now look. Uncle M couldn't have been do-

ing anything wrong, not even gambling. It has to be the Underground."

"Has to be?" Peter knew she was right, just like he knew
Henrik had been right about this. Still, he had a hard time imag-
ining his uncle sneaking around.

"Yes, has to be. The Swedish man was a contact, and Uncle
Morten probably helps to ferry people and things back and
forth. The money we saw was to help pay for gas and things."

Peter thought it sounded right. But how could she be so sure?
And even if their uncle was involved in it somehow, there was
no way he would ever tell them. It would be too dangerous for
anyone to know, especially his family.

"Okay," he admitted. "Maybe you're right. But so what? We
better not say anything about it to anyone. And besides, we'll
probably never know for sure."

"Maybe not," she agreed, "but at least we have a good idea."

Peter didn't say anything for a while, and Elise fidgeted by
the door. She kept glancing toward the living room, where their
parents were still talking quietly.

"I don't really like to think about it, Elise," said Peter finally.
"But I'm glad you figured it out." He was—kind of.

"Yeah," she sighed. "Well, good-night." She closed the door
quietly and padded down the hall to her room.

"Good-night, sis. Thanks." *Elise the detective*, thought Peter. *I
wish she would figure out why Mom and Dad are so grouchy all the
time.*

Not all the time, but it was true that their parents didn't smile
or joke much anymore. Mr. Andersen worried a lot, and he
yelled a lot more than he used to. Mrs. Andersen fussed about
their food. It was like a dark cloud was hanging over their
kitchen table much of the time. Peter put down his book and fell
asleep, trying not to think about the war . . . again.

6

Tangled Up

With the fall came school, war or no war. For Peter, Elise, and Henrik that meant there were only the weekends for biking and hiking around, taking the pigeons out for trips, being kids. And even though they had their ideas, they still hadn't figured out who the Swede in the woods was, or exactly why Uncle Morten was meeting him there. At least not for sure.

Peter didn't think about that as he walked to the boathouse before school. It was his turn to feed the birds and check their water. Even though it was still only September, he could see his breath that morning, and he pretended he was a steam train as he walked down to the waterfront. As usual, his grandfather was puttering around in the shed.

"Morning, Grandpa," he called as he pushed open the door. Peter's grandfather looked up from his perch on a barrel. Like any good fisherman—even though he was mostly retired—he worked a lot on his nets and ropes, things like that. Peter measured out five handfuls of hard corn from the big sack on a shelf, then checked the water bowl. Grandfather had built a cover for the bowl so the birds wouldn't mess it up or tip it over, and they could stick their little necks in to get a drink. Pigeons are one of the only birds that can drink out of their beaks like a straw, which Peter always thought was fun to watch. Most other birds have to get a mouthful and tip it back to drink.

The birds fluttered around Peter's feet as he tiptoed around the coop. He could see they were going to have to do some serious cleaning pretty soon.

"Hey, Peter," said Grandfather as Peter finished his chore. "Your uncle needs a crewman or two to help him this weekend." He cleared his throat. "And I can't make it. Just a few hours tomorrow. Saturday. Short trip. You available?"

Who was he kidding? Peter had wanted to go out with his uncle and grandfather for as long as he could remember. But his parents had never let him—yet—and he had really never been asked. "Sure, Grandpa," he replied, "but—"

"I already talked to your father," he interrupted. "And we agreed you were old enough to go out this time. You won't be staying out overnight or anything. Your uncle leaves at six-thirty."

"Fantastic!" yelled Peter, closing the door to the coop. Then he stopped short. "But what about Elise and Henrik? You think his parents would let him come, too?"

"That's up to them. You can ask. Elise can come, too, if she wants. I'm just not sure if she does. Ask her at school today." Peter's grandfather smiled, then waved Peter out the door. "Out with you now, or you'll be late for school."

"School. Oh, yeah." Peter remembered that Henrik would be waiting for him by the big Saint Mary's church, a couple of blocks from school. Now he would have to run to make it on time—as usual. "I'll be here first thing in the morning. Six o'clock."

"Don't be late," Grandfather called after him as Peter ran out the door. "Your uncle will be waiting for you."

Peter hardly heard. *Wait until I tell Henrik and Elise!*

He met up with Henrik at the church, where the other boy was waiting impatiently.

"What took you so long?" asked Henrik, kicking a pebble down the street.

"I had to talk to Grandfather about something," said Peter. "He asked if we wanted to go out on the boat Saturday."

Henrik's eyes grew wide. "No kidding? And it's okay with your folks?"

"He said he already talked with them and everything, and that if it's okay with your parents . . ."

Henrik winced. "I don't know, Peter. But we can try. You know how my parents are. What about your sister?"

"Did someone mention my name?" said Elise, who had just run up behind the boys on her way down the street. As usual, she had an armload of books, too many to keep in her red school backpack. She had Mrs. Becker, the other fifth-grade teacher, in the classroom next to Henrik's and Peter's.

Henrik wheeled around, surprised. Elise usually walked to school with her girl friends. "Oh, it's you," he said.

"Of course it's me," said Elise, in a teasing manner. "So what did you mean, 'What about your sister?' "

"Grandpa just asked me this morning when I was feeding the birds if we wanted to go out on their boat tomorrow," said Peter. "He said Mom and Dad told him it was okay."

"Great!" she said, pulling at the strap of her backpack while she balanced her extra books in the other hand. "But do you think Henrik's parents will say yes?" She looked quickly over at Henrik, who was kicking the pebble again.

"Maybe," said Peter, feeling hopeful. He was already thinking of all the foot-long herring his uncle and grandfather sometimes returned with. The little silvery fish were everybody's favorite, pickled and sliced on dark rye bread. It was something every Dane learned to eat, almost before they could walk.

"Yeah, and maybe Mr. Jensen will cancel school today and give us a big party," said Henrik. He was smiling, but he and Peter both knew his chances were slim.

Elise ran on ahead. Henrik and Peter made it to school—a large, three-story brick building on King Street—just as the principal, Mr. Jensen, was closing the doors.

"Just in time again, boys," he observed in his big bass-drum voice. They made it to their classroom on the second floor just as the bell rang.

"No party," whispered Henrik, as they slipped into their seats.

No sooner had he sat down than Peter began daydreaming of going out on the boat the next day. He still couldn't believe it—not having to talk his parents into anything. *Incredible.* The only bad part was not knowing if Henrik was going to be able to come. And what about Elise?

Their teacher, Mr. Isaksen, began with math, but Peter was already far out to sea, dreaming. *Maybe we'll bring back enough fish to give Mom some extra, too. All the way out there on the water. Feeling the waves. And if I can steer the boat . . .*

When Peter looked up, everyone seemed to be staring at him. Even Henrik, sitting at the desk just across the aisle, was giving him a strange look.

"The answer, Peter?" Mr. Isaksen crossed his arms and looked straight at Peter. Behind him, Annelise Kastrup giggled, and he could feel the back of his neck heating up, the way it always did when he embarrassed himself. Desperately, he tried to focus back on the real world, tried hard to think of the teacher's question, but he was afraid to ask him to repeat it. Something about fish?

"Umm . . . one hundred herring?" Peter blurted out before he knew what was happening. *Stupid. Why did I say that?* Everybody broke out laughing, except Mr. Isaksen. It only made him look even more serious, more stern.

"That's enough, class," said the teacher. He hardly moved his lips, they were so tightly pressed together—kind of like he was doing a talking puppet routine. His look seemed to drill a hole in Peter. "You may think that was a clever answer, Mr. Andersen, but we are talking about fractions today. You will stay after school this afternoon, please, to brush up on the subject, since you obviously need the practice."

"Yes, sir," said Peter, not looking up.

Peter wanted to melt through the floor, and the back of his neck felt lobster red. Staying after school would only keep him from getting out to the boat and helping get it ready for the next day. He was in a daze all the rest of the morning until lunchtime, but luckily he wasn't called on again.

"Where were you during math today?" Henrik asked when they were eating their lunch in the small school auditorium. Elise usually ate with her friends Tina or Susan. "You looked like you were in outer space or something when Mr. Isaksen asked you that question."

Peter didn't know what to say, really. Besides, Keld Poulsen and Jesper Jarl—the two people who gave him more pain than anyone else in the world—were sitting just down the bench from Peter and Henrik. Peter could tell as they scooted over close that they were coming in for the kill.

"Hey, Andersen," snickered Keld. "Where did you get the hundred herring from? That was a bird-brained answer."

He and his sidekick Jesper were real good at making people feel dumb, like now. Peter knew his face was probably going to get red all over again, and then Jesper would chime in for the second punch. Jesper was just as little and skinny as Keld was big and beefy, and he always copied everything Keld did. *Quite a team*, thought Peter. *Obnoxious.* Just then Peter was wishing he and Henrik had skipped lunch and headed straight for the yard by the side of the building.

"Not a bird-brained answer, Keld," said Jesper, sounding

like the second half of a bad comedy team. "A *pigeon*-brained answer." They were just warming up, daring Henrik or Peter to fight back.

"Hey, who asked you, Jesper?"

Surprised, Keld and Jesper whirled around on the bench to see who was challenging them. Peter knew the voice without looking up but couldn't believe it. *Elise!* She had buzzed in at those two like a hornet, and when the stocky Keld stood up to face his attacker, they were practically nose to nose. But Elise wasn't going to let anyone get a word in edgeways. With her hands on her hips, she lit into him like a drill sergeant.

"You don't know the first thing about birds, anyway," she said. By now, everyone on that side of the room was listening. Peter guessed Keld and Jesper were as surprised as anyone, including himself. "And if you had any birds, they would probably . . . probably fly away from you as fast . . ."

This war of words might have gotten serious if the school's air-raid siren hadn't sounded just then, drowning out the rest of what Elise was saying. She looked around the room like the rest of the lunch crowd, as if expecting to see planes through the ceiling. In a moment Mr. Isaksen took charge.

"Everyone down to the cellar, please," boomed the teacher when the siren dimmed for a moment. "Line up at the door."

Everyone picked up their lunches and started shuffling toward the door, while the wail of the siren went on. They had done this before. But no matter how many times he heard it, the rising and falling wail always gave Peter the shivers. All he wanted to do was plug his ears . . . and be somewhere else.

They would spend the next few minutes, or maybe hours, in the school's cellar until the steady sound of the all-clear siren. Actually, it wasn't too bad because it gave them a chance to read or catch up on homework. No one even cried anymore, the way the younger kids had during the first one or two years of the war. They just lined up by the teacher with his hand in the air, chattering as if there were no British planes flying over on their way to bomb Germany.

Peter thought about it, though, and he didn't like the thought. Only once in a while did bombs fall on their own country, on special German targets. Still, it made him nervous. One thing he was sure of, though: It got very stuffy in the cellar with all the kids down there.

In all the excitement, Peter had almost forgotten about Keld. The boy was red, as if steam was pouring out of his ears, but he didn't say a word until he brushed past Peter.

"When you're least expecting it, Andersen," he half shouted, straight into Peter's ear. Even the constant sound of the siren didn't drown his voice out. "When you don't have a girl to stick up for you . . . you'll wish you weren't alive."

Peter pretended he couldn't hear him. But when he looked back to find Elise, she was gone. *I'll thank her tonight, when I get the chance.* Actually, except for the fear that Keld would probably jump him in an alley someday and knock him silly, Peter didn't mind whoever wanted to stand up against Keld and Jesper. It had just surprised him that it was his own sister. Then Henrik brought him back to reality.

"Come on, Peter," he said, tugging at his friend's shirt. "Are you going to stand there dreaming all day? We have to get down to the air-raid cellar."

The cellar was just like another classroom, really, only there were no windows, and it was only big enough for the whole school—all two hundred kids—to cram into. Peter and Henrik found seats with the rest of their class and took the reading books that were being passed around. It was a spooky feeling being down in the cellar. The sound of the siren somewhere above them made it worse.

It was a short stay this time, though. They had hardly gotten their books open when the steady all-clear siren sounded, and it was time to go back up to their normal classrooms.

"That was quick, don't you think?" Henrik poked Peter as they passed back their books. "The Brits must have been just passing through again."

"Yeah, they must have," Peter replied, but his mind wasn't on air raids. The rest of the afternoon, Peter had to pinch himself a couple of times to keep with it—to not daydream about fishing boats or worry about being attacked by bullies. *Only two more hours.* He looked up at the clock in their classroom as Mr. Isaksen droned on about a spelling test. *Make that two and a half—until school's out at three-thirty. No more bird-brained answers. Just stay with it.*

Henrik was waiting in the school yard when Peter finally came out that afternoon. *Good old Henrik.* He looked as if he was still excited about what had happened at lunch.

"Hey, that was some speech from your sister, wasn't it?" Henrik asked as the two jogged along the street. "Elise scared the socks off old Keld and Jesper."

"Uh-huh." Peter was thinking about old Keld and Jesper jumping out of an alley, so he kept an eye out as they slowed to a walk.

"I mean, I was impressed, weren't you?" Henrik went on. "Did you see the way Keld just stood there and took it, before the air raid? His ears turned beet red."

"I saw."

Henrik obviously hadn't heard Keld's last message, but Peter wasn't going to say anything else. *Maybe Keld will forget all about it*, thought Peter, looking carefully around the corner. *But maybe not. Anyway, if I'm going to live past today, I had better keep an eye out.* They continued on silently until they reached the door to Henrik's little apartment on Star Street, next door to the neighborhood pawn shop.

Theirs looked like so many others in the city, a neatly painted narrow black door with numbers and a small brass plate. "E. Melchior." Henrik took the stairs three at a time, with Peter right on his heels. In the tiny living room, where Mrs. Melchior was folding laundry, Henrik dumped his books on the couch. She looked a lot like her son, or her son like her—dark haired, attractive, with sharp features.

"Hello, Mother, guess what?" Henrik asked in the same breath.

"Come in, and don't leave your books on the couch," she answered. She smiled at Peter.

"Mother, Peter's dad said it's okay with them. Can I go, too?"

"If I knew what Mr. Andersen said okay about, I could answer you better," she said, looking up from a pair of socks she was folding.

"Oh, yeah," said Henrik. He was catching his breath. "Fishing. Going out on their boat. Just for a day. We'd be back before dark. Peter's going."

"I'm not so sure, Henrik," said his mother. "That's something we'll have to discuss with your father tonight when he gets home from work."

"Thanks, Mother. He'll say yes, won't he?" Henrik was a pretty good salesman when he wanted to be.

"We'll have to see about that."

That's about what Henrik and Peter had expected, and it was better than a flat-out no. There was no time to lose, though, so they ran on to Peter's apartment, three blocks away, where Peter dumped his books.

"I'll be back for dinner, Mom," said Peter. "Uncle Morten just needs a little help getting the boat ready so we can leave first thing tomorrow morning. So bye." He finished his sentence as the door slammed behind them. He thought his mother said, "Dinner five-thirty." Something like that. *Or was it six?*

Down at the harbor, Uncle Morten had the floorboards of the fishing boat pulled up and stacked all over the wheelhouse, and the engine in the bottom of the small boat was in pieces. Grandfather was there, too, up to his waist in engine parts. He looked like one of those Greek mythological characters, half boat engine on the bottom and half person on the top. His sleeves were rolled up, and his hands and wrists were black with grease.

"Try it again, Morten," he said to his son. Peter's uncle was at the spoked wooden wheel, perched above the engine and balancing on a couple of beams where the floorboards used to be. He punched the big black starter button next to the wheel. Nothing happened. No click, no whir, no sound. Uncle Morten looked up long enough from what he was doing to flash a smile as Henrik and Peter climbed onto the boat.

"Hey, boys," he said. "You're just in time to help us get some things loaded while we fix this starter." He looked down at his father again. "That is, if we *can* fix this starter. Think you can go back up to the shed and fetch those three piles of rope by the workbench? There's a lot more."

"Sure," said Henrik. Peter climbed after him back up the ramp that led down to the boat dock.

"Hey, these ropes are heavier than I thought," Peter grunted as they struggled with one pile. The ropes were hard to get a handle on. As his grandfather would say, it was like trying to put socks on an octopus.

Trip after trip the boys struggled with those piles of rope, and then fishing floats, tools, and extra parts Uncle Morten directed them to bring down to the boat. Elise arrived a few minutes later and helped with a few loads as well. The three of them were picking up the last load in the boathouse when they heard the roar of the boat engine down on the dock. They looked at one another and cheered, then piled everything that was left into their arms. Peter could hardly see over the top of his armload, and by the time they were halfway down the ramp, he heard the engine shut down again. He looked over his load to see a man in a gray uniform standing by the boat. It was not a Danish policeman.

Without thinking, he froze in fright, and Henrik (with the

same kind of load in his arms) bumped hard into him from the rear. In one scary moment Peter felt himself tumbling down the ramp headfirst. They turned into a tangle of arms, legs, a mop, buckets, a piece of rope, and a spare part for the engine, and they couldn't stop until they were lying in a heap at the German soldier's mirror-shiny high boots. He didn't move an inch, as if he were daring the boys to crash into him. Elise stood helplessly at the top of the ramp, her eyes wide with horror. At the bottom of the heap, Henrik let out a shriek of pain but stopped abruptly when he saw the German. It sounded as if a big hand had clamped hard over his mouth.

Peter didn't want to look up, but he had to, and he saw a frowning German officer, looking down his nose at a tangle of boys and boat stuff.

"Who are these two?" the officer demanded. His Danish sounded mainly like German, but Peter could tell he wasn't fooling around.

"Just my grandson and his friend," Grandfather explained. "They're helping get the boat ready, putting in some supplies. Are you all right, boys?"

The officer didn't wait for Peter or Henrik to answer. "I see that," he snipped. He was probably Uncle Morten's age, tall, straight, and dark haired. He was standing as if he wore a board under the back of his gray wool uniform. One hundred percent serious. The only thing that looked out of place was his crooked nose, which had obviously been broken somewhere along the line. "Are they regular crew members?"

"No," replied Grandfather. "They're just kids."

The two boys untangled themselves and tried to pick up some of the mess, the stuff that was scattered all over the dock. Elise tiptoed quietly down the ramp to help. A mop was floating in the water next to the dock, and she fished it up. Henrik had a strange expression on his ash-colored face, and he was sweating like crazy. Peter was pretty nervous, too—even more nerv-

ous than the time they had let the pigeons go at the Marienlyst
Hotel. He was thinking about Henrik the Jew again.

Then Peter looked back up at his grandfather, searching for
some kind of encouragement. Uncle Morten was behind him,
wiping his hands on a rag. He winked at his nephew.

"So you will report anything you see," said the officer to the
men, still standing in the same spot. "Immediately." It was not
a question.

"We'll keep our eyes open. You'll be the first to hear," said
Uncle Morten. He didn't sound too convincing. "If criminals are
sneaking around, as you say, we have no need for them."

Peter couldn't believe his ears, but he didn't say anything.
In a moment the German swiveled on his toe and walked quickly
up the ramp.

"He's gone," said Uncle Morten, after they had all watched
the gray uniform disappear. That's when Peter and Elise looked
over at Henrik, who was making a funny little whimper. His
knees folded under him, and he fainted quietly onto the dock.

Uncle Morten vaulted out of the boat past Grandfather; everyone crowded around Henrik and tried to lay him on his back.

"Henrik!" yelled Peter. "What's going on?"

"Don't yell at him," snapped Elise. "He fainted and he can't
hear you anyway."

Henrik wasn't answering right away, but it was only a few
moments before his eyes fluttered open again. Uncle Morten
wadded a jacket and placed it under his head, and Grandfather
covered him with another coat he had found in the boat.

"My arm. My arm. My arm!" Tears were streaming down his
face.

Uncle Morten touched Henrik's arm where there was a
lump, and the boy yelped. Uncle Morten looked up. "It's probably broken," he said. "But I can't believe you didn't say anything until now. Why not?"

Henrik tried to catch his breath. "I couldn't say anything

while he was here," he choked. "I just couldn't."

"Well, let's get you up to a doctor," said Grandfather. "This is going to take some looking after. Can you walk?"

He could—barely—and Uncle Morten put his arm around the boy's waist as he guided him down the street to the neighborhood clinic on Star Street. But the arm, Henrik's left arm, did turn out to be broken.

"It's not so bad that it won't heal just fine," said Dr. Rasmussen, closing up his bag. He had just finished putting a small cast on Henrik's forearm. Henrik said the pain was still terrific, but with his parents around he was grinning anyway from where he sat on the clean hospital bed. He smiled at the doctor, Uncle Morten, Grandfather, Elise, and Peter. He had a small audience in the clinic room, and Henrik was performing.

"So, Doctor, will I be able to play the piano after my arm heals?" Henrik asked.

"No, Mr. Melchior," replied the doctor, straight-faced. "Not unless you start taking lessons."

"Aw, you didn't fall for it," said Henrik.

"I've heard that one before," the doctor replied, looking down at his clipboard. He was smiling, though. "Take very good care of this arm for a month or so. No tumbling or arm wrestling; keep the activity down. And come back in six weeks."

"Thanks so much, Doctor," said Mrs. Melchior.

Then Henrik suddenly frowned. "This means I won't be able to go out with Peter and his uncle tomorrow on the boat, right?"

Henrik's dad had already heard about the trip. Now he looked even more serious than he usually did, and his black, bushy eyebrows were bunched close down over his eyes. He was rather short and stubby looking, not at all athletic like his son. And the decision about the fishing trip was already made for him now. "I think you know the answer to that, son," he said. "I'm sorry. You heard the doctor."

Henrik groaned. Then he looked at his friends. "But you'll go anyway, right, Peter? Elise?"

Peter wasn't so sure. Since the tumble on the dock, he felt all jumbled inside. He felt terrible about Henrik getting hurt, and how he made him fall, even though it was an accident. But Henrik hadn't even let anyone apologize. *At least he isn't mad at me,* thought Peter. He remembered what his uncle had said to the German officer, and that was bothering him, too. None of it fit; none of it seemed right. He had a giant headache.

"Right, Peter?" Henrik repeated.

"Well, I guess so," replied Peter, not really knowing what he was saying. "If Uncle Morten is still going out." It wouldn't be quite as fun, Henrik at home with a broken arm, but yes, he still did want to go out.

"I'm planning on it, Peter," said Uncle Morten. "We still have to go out and make a living, even though I'm not planning a long day tomorrow. The fish are waiting." Then he turned to Elise. "And what about you, young lady—you're coming, too?"

Elise looked down, then over at her uncle. "I . . . I can't," she said hesitantly. "You and Peter will have fun. Maybe I can go out next time." Obviously embarrassed, she turned and ran outside.

Uncle Morten looked puzzled, but just shrugged and turned to Henrik's father.

"I'm very sorry it happened this way," said Morten. "Your son was helping us, but it was an accident. The boys weren't horsing around or anything."

"Oh, I realize that fully." Mr. Melchior waved his hand, dismissing the situation. "And no one is blaming you. These things happen sometimes." He sounded polite and calm, but at the same time he pulled out his handkerchief and wiped the sweat off his forehead. Peter wasn't sure whether he was upset about Henrik getting hurt, or about the German down on the dock. The officer had been looking for something. Or someone.

Before Peter left for home, he saw Mr. Melchior and Uncle Morten move back to a corner of the clinic, behind a cabinet full of bandages and supplies. Mr. Melchior was gesturing—not mad, but making a point. Peter's uncle put his hand on the other man's shoulder and said something else to him. Peter didn't want to seem too nosy, so he didn't stare. But as everyone left, the two men were still in the corner, whispering. Uncle Morten looked up and waved to Peter.

"Tomorrow early, right?" he said.

"Six o'clock," Peter called back as he headed out, looking for Elise.

"Wait a minute," said Henrik as Peter was just about to close the door. "I have an idea. Why don't you send a message back with Number Two?"

Peter thought for just a second, then brightened a bit. "Sounds great! Check the boathouse with Elise at three or four o'clock to see if the bird's made it back."

"I'll make it out of the sickbed for that, at least," Henrik laughed as Peter left.

Peter found Elise outside the clinic, and they walked home together, neither of them saying a word. He wanted to say something that might make her feel better, but couldn't.

7

ON THE SOUND

"Henrik and Elise should be here," Peter said to his uncle as they headed out of the harbor.

Henrik couldn't help it, of course, but Elise had just told her brother again the night before that she would rather not go. Something about "all those smelly fish." Peter couldn't understand why she was turning down this chance that he'd been waiting for for so long. Even though they were twins, there were some things about Elise he just couldn't figure out.

Looking around at the ocean, Peter decided she was silly to be missing all this. The water on the Sound was almost like a mirror that morning, reflecting all the way to Sweden. Only the long, low swells turned it into a kind of soft cake frosting, and the *Anna Marie* rode the frosting like a rocking horse finding its place in the world. It would have been enough to put Peter to sleep if he hadn't been so excited about being out there.

"Here, you take the wheel for a while," said Uncle Morten. He pointed out familiar landmarks that would help them stay on course. A church steeple in the little coastal town of Julebaek on the Danish side. A strange hill over on the Swedish side, taller than the rest. A bright red buoy, usually covered with gulls. Peter almost forgot what had happened the day before, until a gray German patrol boat appeared from behind, coming fast.

"Watch," said Uncle Morten, keeping track of the boat out of the corner of his eye as it got closer. It was speeding through the gentle swells, throwing out spray. "I'll bet they're going to stop us."

They didn't, but they came close. Two sailors with dark blue uniforms stood on deck and stared straight at the *Anna Marie*. They looked like two college kids out for a boat ride, only they obviously weren't having fun. No one was smiling. No one waved either, and the little fishing boat bobbed in the wake of the patrol boat as it sped by. Peter looked down, and his knuckles were white. He eased his grip on the wheel and took a deep breath. Seeing the German boat reminded him about the conversation on the dock the day before. The question kept nagging at him. *How can I ask Uncle Morten without sounding like I'm accusing him of being a German spy?*

"Hey, Uncle Morten," Peter finally said, looking for the right approach. "Umm ... can I ... can I ask you about what happened yesterday?"

Morten turned his head, his eyebrows raised. "What, besides your friend breaking his arm?"

"You know, when the German guy was at the boat and we fell down the gangway and you and Grandpa were talking to the guy and you told him something about keeping an eye out for him, helping to catch smugglers or criminals, you didn't have any need for criminals, did you really mean that or what?" It all spilled out at once in one long sentence.

His uncle looked ahead through the wheelhouse window, and he smiled a long, easy smile. Then he looked over again, and there was a twinkle in his eye. "How long have you known me, Peter?" he finally asked.

"You know. All my life. Except for when you were fishing in Iceland."

"Okay. Now, do you have any idea how I feel about the Germans coming in and taking over our country?"

"Well, I thought I did, but that's what I can't figure out. I can't even imagine that you would work with the Germans, but you never talk about it much, especially after we saw you giving all that money to the Swedish guy in the woods."

Peter bit his tongue. He hadn't meant to say anything about the meeting in the woods, especially not about seeing the money.

"I mean, I mean, really," Peter continued. "Why don't you . . ."

Uncle Morten didn't change his expression. "Why don't I what? Cooperate with the Nazis? Are you joking?"

"No, why don't you talk about it that much?"

Uncle Morten took a deep breath, and the smile faded. "I'm not trying to keep secrets, Peter, really. But it's just better that . . . well . . . let me start over." There was a pause. "I really can't tell you that much about what I do, not even about the Swedish fellow. I'm sorry. But I can promise you that I'll explain the whole thing to you after the war is over."

The fisherman stared at a gull gliding by the boat, and chewed his tongue. "Listen," he said, finally. "I don't know how to explain things other than sometimes we find ourselves in the awkward spot of having to mislead someone—the enemy—to protect something else, something very valuable."

"So you didn't mean what you said to the German yesterday, about helping him out?"

Uncle Morten blew out through his teeth with a kind of "har-umph."

"Things aren't always the way they seem, Peter." His lips were tight and serious looking as he said it. "And I dislike dealing this way with anyone, for any reason. But these people are out to destroy. . . . They're out to destroy everyone and everything that's good and important to this country." His face was getting red now, and his voice sounded different.

Peter looked straight at him, a little surprised. He had never heard his uncle, normally cool and mild, so heated up. They were quiet for another minute, two minutes.

When Uncle Morten spoke again, he was cooling down. "You understand what I just said?"

"I'm not sure, Uncle Morten." Peter wasn't, but he was starting to get an idea. "All I wanted to know was what you were talking about with that German officer. I didn't mean anything by it, really. I'm just kind of confused."

"And maybe you still are, and maybe I said too much." He laughed again, the old Uncle Morten. "Look, I don't want to confuse things any more, so let me say it straight for you. Since I've become a Christian a few years ago, I've learned that it's wrong to lie, period. The Bible says so. But the Bible also tells the story of a woman who hid two Jewish spies during a war, and then she lied to the authorities about which way they went."

"And that was okay?" Peter asked, feeling like some kind of Bible student.

"Well, the story was in the Old Testament, in the Book of Joshua. Later on, in the New Testament, there's mention of the woman again. And it says she did the right thing."

"I'm not saying you did the wrong thing, Uncle Morten, I just . . ."

"I know, Peter. And I didn't want to give you a complicated answer to a simple question. I just wanted you to know."

"I think I'm getting it now," said Peter. Mainly, he was relieved to hear that Uncle Morten wasn't on the wrong side. Not that he ever believed it. And even though Uncle Morten hadn't come straight out and said so, the message was clear. Elise and Henrik had been right. Uncle Morten was in the Underground, and the money had probably been for smuggling people across to Sweden or something like that. At that point Peter guessed it was none of his business.

But this was a day of surprises. It made Peter wonder, and he smiled inside when he thought about how his uncle was sharing so much about himself, even the Bible things. After all, he didn't have a wife to talk to, even though Peter knew his uncle had a lot of church friends.

Peter learned a few other things that morning, mostly about fishing, steering a straight line, finding out where the fish were. He steered, while Morten did most of the work out on the deck. Peter's uncle said they were having a "vacation" day, not worrying too much about a serious catch. *Fine with me,* thought Peter. *Just being out here on the water is good enough.* And now that he knew more about Uncle Morten, he wasn't as worried. Relieved, more. He made a note to himself that he would have to tell Elise and Henrik, as soon as he got a chance.

"So when are you going to let the bird go?" Uncle Morten asked around lunchtime. He paused for a minute to look up from a net.

The bird! Peter had completely forgotten about Number Two after he had stashed her in the wicker fishing basket and put her underneath the small counter in the back of the *Anna Marie*'s wheelhouse. He was sure she was okay, but she hadn't made a sound all morning.

"Oh, yeah!" said Peter. "What message should we send?" He reached into his pocket and pulled out the small capsule with the snap strap, the one that went around the bird's leg.

"How about, 'Heading south. All is well. Catching lots of fish. Peter and Morten.' Think that's too long?"

"No, just right." Peter braced himself against the side of the wheelhouse while he scribbled on a scrap of paper torn from a little black notebook Uncle Morten kept in the boat. Then he pulled out the bird and checked her over. In a minute, the message was rolled up tight and secure in the capsule and on the homing pigeon's leg.

They both watched after Peter tossed the bird into the clear sky above the boat. As usual, she circled twice, her wings whistling and flap-clapping together with the musical sound that only pigeons make. Peter never got tired of watching. Something about it. In a minute, her built-in compass kicked in, and she turned north and headed straight for home, for Helsingor—their city of steeples, shipyard cranes, brick buildings, and Kronborg Castle.

"She'll be home in a half hour," said Peter, straining to see Number Two as she disappeared in the distance.

"Right," said Uncle Morten. "That's a pretty good way to send your airmail. Doesn't even need a stamp." Now he was finished with his net, and he popped a hard-boiled egg into his mouth. Peter's mom would never let him do anything like that at home, so he tried it, too. He almost gagged, it was so big.

The rest of the afternoon fell into a pattern. Peter steered, and Uncle Morten let out net. Uncle Morten pulled in net, and Peter steered some more. Peter wasn't sure how his uncle ever did it by himself, but they were catching a few fish this day, and his uncle said he was a big help. They both picked out and threw back the unwanted fish—big ugly things with bulging eyes, spiny backs, flapping gills. They kept the little herring, and the hold—the big storage bin in the middle of the boat—was getting fuller. It was hard work, and Peter's hands and arms were aching. But they were out on the water. Sometimes they didn't say anything; other times Peter's uncle answered all his questions. What's this for? Why are we doing that? How do you know?

Mostly they talked about regular things—the fish, the boat, the weather, the waves. But what Peter really wanted to know was something different. Something about what his uncle had said when he was explaining about the Germans, right after he had gotten all upset. Peter kept it to himself as long as he could.

If I ask, he might start talking about his strange little church, or about the Bible, the way Grandfather does so much. He wanted to hear, but he didn't. He wondered, but he didn't want to know. He was interested but a little afraid to show it. He had been to church— the big Lutheran church in the middle of the city—enough times to know the language. *So why not ask?*

Something made him blurt out a question, almost before he really knew what it was.

"I was just curious, Uncle Morten," Peter finally said. Uncle Morten had just played out the net again, and he looked up with his usual grin. He was a lot like Henrik that way.

"What? Philosophy, politics, the war, or how to save the world?"

"No, really, what you said before, when we were talking about the Germans."

"Oh." He looked out over the water toward Sweden, now a blue-green blur in the distance as they headed south into the open waters of the Sound. He cocked his head at his nephew, looking up with one eye. "Look, I don't know how much more I can tell you about that. I've already said too—"

"No, not about the Germans," Peter interrupted. "Or about what you do in the Under—" He bit his tongue again. "It's what you said about becoming a Christian."

Peter felt himself asking the questions, but it was almost as if it *wasn't* him. He had avoided it pretty well before. "I mean, I'm just curious, a little. I know you go to that little house-church, and all those other meetings, but you've always been a Christian, right?"

At that, Uncle Morten leaned up against the pilothouse, threw back his head, and laughed, big.

"What's so funny?" Peter asked, suddenly feeling dumb. It wasn't that strange a question, but his uncle just kept laughing.

"I'm sorry," he finally said, catching his breath. "No, it's really not a strange or funny question."

"I didn't think so." Peter was regretting that he had opened his big mouth.

"Really, I didn't mean anything," Uncle Morten said. "I'm sorry to laugh. It's just that Arne, I mean your father, asked me exactly the same question, in exactly those words, when I told him I had become a Christian."

"Was that before you and Grandpa took me to that prayer meeting?"

"You remember that?" He smiled. "Good. I wasn't ever sure if we scared you off or something, because you didn't say anything about it afterward. But anyway, yes, it was just a couple of months before that meeting when I committed my life to Jesus."

"Oh," said Peter. "Well, that makes sense . . . kind of." Of course, he had always considered *himself* a Christian, too. He was baptized when he was a baby, like everyone else he knew, except Henrik. Peter figured that if anyone had a chance at getting to heaven, he probably did, too. No murders or robberies on his record.

"Kind of?" asked Uncle Morten. "It didn't make sense to me for a long time. Almost all my life, in fact. I thought I was a Christian way before that."

"But you weren't? How could you tell?"

"Listen," said Uncle Morten. He pulled off his gloves and looked straight at Peter. "I don't want to sound preachy to you, and that's why I've never told you this before. But since you asked, maybe this is the right time." He paused for a second, watching for Peter's reaction.

"I'm listening, Uncle Morten," he said. It was his turn to be nervous, but now there was no longer any question. He wanted to hear the rest of the story.

"Okay, then, here's what happened: I met this guy, Knud Kvist, another fisherman, and there was something very different about him. He went to this little church I'm going to now. I ended up asking him about the same questions you're asking me now. Basically, he told me that I wasn't a Christian because I went to church once in a while, or because I was baptized, or because I believed in God, or not even because I did the right things most of the time."

"So what's left?" Peter went down the list in his head, trying to think of anything that was missing. He couldn't think of anything.

Uncle Morten grinned. "Kvist told me that to follow Jesus—to become a Christian—we need to confess our sins and surrender our whole selves to Christ. Becoming a Christian means realizing that you can't get to heaven by being good. So that's my sermon. Does that make sense?"

Peter nodded, doing his best to take it all in. "It makes sense."

Peter didn't have time to think about it much more, though, because it was time for Uncle Morten to turn back to his net, and they were hauling in a pretty big load. That kept the two busy for the next hour, and then it was time to head back. Uncle Morten let Peter take the wheel again, and he tried to keep a straight course back to Helsingor Harbor.

"Keep the steeple straight ahead," said Uncle Morten.

"No problem," said Peter. It was still clear and beautiful, but an afternoon chop had picked up. With the wind from behind, the waves scooted under the boat and tossed it around more than earlier in the day. All the things Peter's uncle had told him felt like waves, too, knocking his head silly. He had heard it all before, but somehow it had never registered. *What if Uncle Morten is right about this Jesus thing?*

"You're all over the place, Peter," said Uncle Morten, interrupting Peter's thoughts. He had been zigzagging. Morten put his big hand on the wheel to help straighten them out.

"Sorry," said Peter, lining up on his bearing again. But he was still thinking. *Uncle Morten said I haven't really been a Christian all this time. At least, I think that's what he was saying. . . .*

Peter tried to keep his attention on steering, on the waves. A larger wave slipped under the boat just then, and he held on tight to keep from falling over. He was thinking, thinking hard, but still doing pretty well at steering a straight course back to the harbor. *Just so he doesn't ask me what I'm thinking. This isn't what I came on the fishing boat to find out about.*

Before Uncle Morten could say anything else, Peter handed him the wheel and escaped out onto the breezy deck. Maybe he could think better out there, he thought, without embarrassing himself.

It took a few minutes, but Peter's heart slowly settled down. The spray in his face from an occasional wandering wave even felt good. Cold, but good. *That's better.* He got as far back as he could on the rear deck of the boat and watched the seagulls behind and above. "Lucky bird," he told one that glided closer to the boat than the rest. "You don't have to worry about anything."

He dug his hands deep into the pockets of his overcoat. He felt a hard bread crust in his right pocket, forgotten there a long time ago. For the birds. Picking out a seagull, Peter leaned over the edge of the boat and heaved the bread crust as hard as he could.

It all happened in an instant. Peter grabbed for something—anything—but only came up with air. The next moment he was coughing on ice-cold salt water, thrashing around, panicky. Only when his head popped up again above the water did Peter realize what was going on, and by that time the fishing boat was already well out of reach.

"Uncle Morten!" he tried to yell, but he was still choking on seawater. His jacket and pants billowed up around him, and it was hard to stay on top of the green waves. The cold made him instantly numb, squeezing the breath out of him.

"Uncle Morten! Hey! HEY!" *Is he just going to sail off without me?* Peter waved with one hand, paddled with the other, and yelled as loudly as he could. *There's no way he can hear me.* Peter panicked, swallowed a salty wave, gagged and spit. The boat was still moving away fast. His best hope now, he thought, would just be to stay afloat as long as he could. Uncle Morten couldn't get far before he would notice Peter was gone. But he would probably have to start stripping off his shoes; his coat was already off. Anything to make it easier to stay up. *Don't panic,* he told himself. Then his teeth started chattering, and he couldn't stop shivering.

He was just unlacing his shoes, bobbing down underwater, coming up for air, when he saw the *Anna Marie.* She was heading straight at Peter, full speed, waves spraying out in front. A moment later two big hands pulled Peter over the rail. He kneeled on the deck, dripping and gasping.

"Take that wet stuff off," ordered Uncle Morten with a no-nonsense voice. Peter obeyed, his teeth still chattering and his body shaking all over from the cold. His uncle pulled out a blanket and a big parka from underneath a seat and wrapped him snuggly. Inside the pilothouse, out of the wind, he started to warm up again.

"I saw you standing back there one minute, and the next second you were gone," said the fisherman, steering once again toward home. "You couldn't have been in the water for more than a minute or two before I pulled around and got you."

"A minute or two?" asked Peter. "It seemed more like an hour. I just panicked when I saw the boat sailing away from me." It was easier to describe now that he was getting warm and dry, or mostly dry.

"So if you wanted to go swimming, you should have told me, Peter." Then he got serious. "Really, though, if you want to go out again, you're going to have to be extra careful around that railing."

Peter nodded and shivered, feeling as if he had almost died.

Then he remembered what he had been thinking about when he fell overboard.

"Warming up?" Uncle Morten's question interrupted his thoughts.

"Uh-huh."

"I think there's an old pair of work clothes under there where I got the blanket. See if you can find them. They won't fit you very well, and they probably smell pretty bad, but it's better than walking home in just a blanket."

Peter nodded, then found a pair of grease-stained pants and a ripped gray shirt under a cork life jacket. They were big—way big—but he put them on. Better than wet clothes for sure. After a few minutes, he started to warm back up.

Uncle Morten kept his course and looked over at Peter. "About what I said earlier, Peter, I'll say one more thing, and then I won't preach at you anymore." Peter looked up at him, but didn't say anything. "If you really want to follow Jesus, it's your move. All you have to do is tell Him so. I won't ever bug you about it."

"Thanks," Peter managed to mumble as his uncle kept the boat on course through the waves. He wasn't quite sure what to think anymore. It all made sense, but. . . . He sat on the seat over the life-jacket box in the corner of the wheelhouse, his knees pulled up to his chest under the huge shirt, and the parka wrapped around his shoulders. He closed his eyes, listened to all the sounds, felt the boat rock. Before Peter knew what was happening, his head was nodding, and he was asleep.

When Peter woke up, the boat had stopped rocking. He sat up with a jerk, trying to figure out where he was. A fisherman friend of Uncle Morten's was tying up the front end of the boat, but Peter couldn't see his uncle.

"Hey, sailor, we're back." There he was, poking his head into the wheelhouse.

"Oh," said Peter, still a little groggy. "I must have fallen asleep."

"Yeah, you really conked out. Must have been all that swimming." Then he looked around for a moment. "Why don't you just go ahead; I have plenty of help here unloading. Besides, you'd trip over yourself in those old clothes." He chuckled. "They're a little big for me, too. I don't know where I got them."

Peter looked down at himself. The shirt was twice as big as he was, and the only way the big pants stayed on was with a cord wrapped two times around. But he had to laugh, too, it looked so silly.

"Well, okay. But I feel pretty stupid walking through town like this. I hope nobody sees me."

"Up to you, Peter. You could change back into your salty, wet clothes." Peter shuddered at the thought but considered it. "Tell your mom and dad that I'll be by in about forty-five minutes. I'll explain to them what happened when you fell in."

"Thanks, Uncle Morten. You saved my life."

"Well, hardly," he smiled. "We're still working on that."

Peter shivered, thinking again about his wet clothes that had wrapped around him like seaweed, about the numbing cold water, and about everything his uncle had told him that afternoon. With his wet clothes rolled up and tucked under his arm, Peter jumped down onto the dock and ran toward home.

8

HOME FOR DINNER

As the pigeon flies, it was only about six city blocks from the harbor to the Andersen home. Eight to Henrik's apartment above the little bookstore on Star Street. First Peter had to check in with the birds, though. He poked his head in the door of the shed and counted: *One, two, three, four, five. . . . All there.* He knew Number Two would make it back just fine.

Now he had to find a quick way home, without being seen by anyone. He tried a few back streets, smaller ones like Mountain Street and Stone Street. It was getting dark, he thought, so maybe no one would see him there. At least he didn't hear anybody laugh yet, but a couple of boys on their bikes—older teenagers—gave him a good stare. *I look like some kind of hobo.* Down Rose Spring Street, past the red brick City Hall with its tall tower and large entryway, around the corner, and Peter was home.

He almost made it to his room, but Elise caught him in the hallway. "So, Peter, who designed your new wardrobe? No, really, it's kind of cute, and the color matches—"

Peter slipped into his room and slammed the door. *Sisters.*

Even though Peter was glad his uncle came by for dinner and explained what happened, Elise still kept grinning the whole time. It was a funny story, but maybe not that funny.

"Hey, don't laugh," he growled at her. "That water was cold."

"But how long were you in the ocean?" asked Mrs. Andersen. She seemed the most concerned, even after Uncle Morten had explained to everybody that he had turned right around and picked up Peter within minutes.

"Really, not long," Uncle Morten explained. He tried again to make everyone understand that it wasn't such a big thing. "It only took me a moment to realize Peter had flipped off the back end, and . . ."

"But how did you get so tipsy, Peter?" asked Elise. At this point, Peter hated having to explain himself.

"I told you," he said again. "I had some bread, and I was just throwing it to the seagulls." That was enough to send off another round of giggles.

"Speaking of birds," said Elise, looking more serious. "Henrik and I were down at the boathouse when Number Two came back, at two-thirty. We got the message you sent. Henrik said to tell you he got it, if he didn't see you first."

"Oh, great," said Peter. "I was going to stop by his house, but I wanted to get straight home instead."

"Because of your outfit, right?" She started to giggle again.

"Come on, Elise. I'm fine."

But he wasn't . . . not really. All the rest of that evening, Peter would feel himself shivering again. He kept thinking about what Uncle Morten had said to him. *Stop shaking,* he told himself as he got ready for bed around eight-thirty.

"Going to bed so early?" his mom asked. "Are you sure you're all right, after that dunking?" She walked over and put her hand on Peter's forehead. He ducked, but she stayed with him.

"I'm fine. Just a little tired."

"Well, it's been a long day for you," she said, "and there's no school tomorrow. You just get a good night's sleep."

"I will, Mom."

Peter almost told her that he felt strange, but there was no reason to get her more worried than she already was. *I'll feel better in the morning.*

He lay awake in bed, listening to everyone else in the apartment. Ten minutes went by. Twenty. An hour. *So much for getting a good night's sleep.* Maybe he couldn't sleep because of the nap he'd had on the boat. He rolled over, pulled up the covers, twitched and scratched. He tried counting pigeons. But no matter what he did, his uncle's voice kept playing over and over again in his head. "If you really want to follow Jesus, it's your move."

He put his pillow over his head, trying to make the thoughts go away, but, of course, they wouldn't. *It's my move.* Finally he fell into a restless sleep.

9

ROSH HASHANAH

"One thing for sure," Henrik announced as he and Peter were washing up for dinner at the Melchiors' apartment later that week. He had a little trouble doing it one-handed, his left arm still in a cast. But he managed all right. It was Thursday night, a school night, and somehow Peter's mom and dad had allowed him to eat over at Henrik's home. Maybe because it was a special Jewish holiday for the Melchiors, and Peter had been invited as the guest of honor. Peter was even going to be able to stay the night, which he didn't understand at all because it wasn't even a weekend. But both their moms had agreed over the phone, so he wasn't going to argue. It was kind of like the way Peter's grandfather had arranged for him to go out on the fishing boat. Strange, but okay.

"One thing for sure," Henrik repeated as they sat down at the small dinner table in one corner of the apartment. "We can't let the dumb old war stop the Great Danish Pigeon Race."

"Oh?" Henrik's dad had just sat down. His mother was bringing steaming dishes of food to the table, and the four of them were ready. "You had better explain that to me after we say the blessing."

Mr. and Mrs. Melchior looked more like brother and sister than husband and wife. They were both short and a little dark, at least darker than most other Danes. Mr. Melchior had a crop of thin black hair, cut short around his ears. Luckily, Mrs. Melchior had a lot more hair than that, though it was the same color. Henrik said once that his great-grandparents had come to Denmark from Portugal, which was why his family looked the way they did.

Mr. Melchior began the blessing. This wasn't an ordinary night for Henrik and his parents, and it wasn't an ordinary meal. It was, for Jewish families, the first day of the New Year celebration, called Rosh Hashanah. Henrik had said that this dinner was the first celebration in a ten-day period that went all the way to something called Yom Kippur. The Day of Atonement. Peter was surprised they had invited him. He had never been to anything like this in the years since the Melchiors had moved to town.

The guest of honor didn't know exactly what was going on, so he just watched. Mr. Melchior looked at Peter, and Peter felt like a tourist visiting the Kronborg Castle for the first time. Henrik's dad was going to show him a place he had never been before, full of history and stories of people he had never met.

"This is the Kaddish, or blessing, that we say before having the wine," explained Mr. Melchior. He held up a sparkling glass with a long, thick stem, and the ruby red wine sloshed around in it. "Blessed are you, O Lord our God, King of the Universe, who creates the fruit of the vine."

After he had said that, Mrs. Melchior passed a plate to him, and he put down the glass for a minute. On the plate was a large loaf of bread—all braided. Then the tour guide looked at Peter again.

"This is a special Jewish bread," he explained, "called hallah.

It's braided and made into a big, round hat shape. A crown. It reminds us of the King." Then he continued with his blessing.

"Blessed are you, O Lord our God, King of the Universe, who brings forth bread from the earth."

Peter was starting to get the idea now about the food. Mrs. Melchior even poured a little splash of wine in small glasses for the two boys. Henrik leaned over and whispered to Peter, "Now comes the good part." Peter didn't know why he whispered, but it was turning out to be that kind of meal. Not in a bad way, but definitely different.

"Well, it wasn't easy to get," said Mr. Melchior with a smile, "but I understand Ruth, Mrs. Melchior, found some honey last June, and saved it all this time." He patted her hand across the table. "Perfect." Then Henrik's dad looked over at Peter again. "There is another blessing to ask before we eat these apple slices dipped in honey." He pointed to a bowl of cut yellow fruit. Peter knew the words by now and was almost following along.

"Blessed are you, O Lord our God, King of the Universe, who creates the fruit of the tree."

Peter followed Henrik's example by taking an apple slice and dipping it into the small dish of honey. *Not bad at all.* When they finished their apples and licked the honey off their lips, Mr. Melchior cleared his throat again. There would be another blessing, or prayer, or something.

"May it be your will, O Lord and God of our Fathers," he recited in his deep voice, "to renew unto us a happy and sweet year."

Mrs. Melchior looked out the window just then, and for a moment she seemed far away. "A happy and sweet year," she repeated softly.

That said, everyone went on to the rest of the dinner, which was more like a traditional wartime meal. Cabbage, a little fish, some small potatoes. Mr. Melchior was even served a steaming fish head, another Jewish holiday tradition for the head of the household. Peter and Henrik were halfway through their cabbage when Mr. Melchior brought up the pigeon race again.

"Now, tell me." He looked up briefly and smiled at his wife; she was spooning another potato onto his plate. "What is all this about the Great Danish Pigeon Race? It's different from what you boys had been doing this summer?" It seemed to Peter that he asked in an interested sort of way, as if he really wanted to know.

"Just a little different, Father," said Henrik, carefully choosing his words. He spoke to his dad almost the same way Peter did to his grandfather, only a little more formally, with a little more respect. His parents were a lot older than Peter's. "Peter and his sister and I have been training the birds to fly home from farther and farther away, you know."

"And I'm not sure I approve anymore," interrupted his father.

What? Peter was afraid Henrik's dad was going to bring up the whole episode down at the boat again, when Henrik broke his arm.

"It was one thing when you boys were just staying around town, and the summer was quieter," continued his dad. "But with all these Germans around now, and the way things are going, it's just not safe anymore. I've spoken to Peter's uncle about this. But," he paused, thinking for a moment, "go ahead and explain it some more for me." Then, without waiting for an answer from his son, he looked straight at Peter. "How is this race any different?"

Peter gulped, caught in the middle now. Henrik's father, a manager in the largest department store downtown, was at the same time stern, friendly, and scary. His mom, on the other hand, was just as shy as Mr. Melchior was outgoing. She was looking at Peter, too, expecting some kind of answer. He had his mouth full of potato.

"Well, sir," he said, sputtering a little, "my uncle Morten is a fisherman, and—"

"Yes, I know your uncle."

Peter knew he knew. He gulped, then continued. "Well, he told me he would take our three birds out sometime and let them start the race from Sweden."

"Sweden?" Mr. Melchior's dark eyebrows went up. He put his fork down, as if trying to figure out what Peter had just said. "And what would he be doing all the way over there? He knows what would happen to him if a German patrol boat found him returning from outside Danish waters, doesn't he?"

Peter felt as if he had just stuck a big foot in his mouth. Not that he knew anything secret about what Uncle Morten was doing, and Mr. Melchior was no friend of the Nazis. But still . . .

"I think he gets out kind of far sometimes," Peter said. "He probably just meant . . ." He didn't know how to finish his sentence without telling a lie. But by then Mrs. Melchior must have seen how he was sweating this one, and she came to the rescue.

"You don't need to say anything else, Peter," she said, her voice soft. "We won't tell anyone where your uncle likes to fish. He's a fine man, and we certainly wouldn't want to see anyone else learn about his . . . well, his fishing secrets." She looked at her husband, sending him a message with her eyes. Peter had seen his own mom give his dad the same look plenty of times before.

"But as for you, young Mister Melchior," said Henrik's dad, "I'm sad to say that you will be staying away from Peter's uncle from here on, for safety's sake." Henrik almost slid under the table. "As your mother said, he's a fine man, and we certainly have nothing against him. It has nothing to do with your arm, either. It's just for safety's sake. And that means keeping your bird out of his boat as well. I'm very sorry."

Peter got the feeling Mr. Melchior was a little embarrassed to be bringing all this up right then, at the Rosh Hashanah meal and all. And Peter didn't want to start a family feud right there, on a holiday. He looked at Henrik to see how he was reacting, and his friend was moving food around on his plate, looking down.

"Are you serious, Father?" said Henrik, questioning his dad for the first time since Peter could remember.

"Quite serious, son. Have you forgotten who we are?"

"You mean do I remember we're Jewish? I'm Danish, too, Father, just like everybody else. Just like Peter."

Mr. Melchior's neck stiffened. If Peter hadn't been at the table with them, he might have exploded.

"Not like everyone else, I'm afraid," said Mr. Melchior, measuring his words carefully. "We're Danes, but we're Jewish Danes. Or Danish Jews. I'm not sure. Those German soldiers outside would love to remind us of it, too."

"Esaias!" Now Henrik's mother interrupted. "There's no need to start into that conversation again. This is a holiday, remember?"

"I think the boys know at least as much as we do, dear." Mr. Melchior swept his hand past the lace curtains on the window and pointed his sharp finger out at the street. "The boys are out there all the time, riding their bicycles and such. The only thing they don't know is how much has happened in the other countries. To Jews. To family." His face was drawn tight now.

"Please, Father," protested Henrik, this time a little less defiant. He had drawn back from the edge of his chair now and was still picking nervously at his plate. "Nobody has ever bothered me about being Jewish. Nobody cares. It's not like any of the stories you've told me. Denmark's different."

Finally Mr. Melchior smiled a little, and he gave a kind of sad chuckle. "You're right, son, a little bit right. We're accepted here, even though we are looking less and less like Jews all the time. But that's another story. The terrible things that are happening to Jews in Poland, in Germany, haven't happened here. We should be thankful to God."

There was a long pause. Peter was hoping Henrik's dad would change his mind about the pigeons, about Uncle Morten . . . maybe if Henrik would stop arguing. But just then, it didn't look good for the Great Danish Pigeon Race.

"That doesn't change the fact that we—this family—we are still Jews," continued Mr. Melchior, "and we live in a place that's been taken over by a German crazyman who hates the Jews. You, Henrik, son of Israel, are not going to go around looking for trouble. That's the end of it. Now, please pass the cabbage, if there's any left that's not ice-cold."

End of discussion. Period. That was it. There would be no pigeon races from Uncle Morten's boat. Henrik looked over at Peter and gave him a look like "What can I do about it?"

Peter just wanted to keep his mouth shut and not get into the argument.

"So tomorrow," Mrs. Melchior tried to brighten things up. "We're all going to the harbor after school, yes?" Henrik nodded, and his mom looked at Peter with her friendly smile again. She was really trying to make him feel more comfortable, especially after this discussion. "Every year, Peter, we follow the same Jewish tradition." Peter nodded. "At the waterfront we empty our pockets of bread crumbs and lint, and we cast it all into the ocean. Jews all over the world do the same thing. When the water carries away the crumbs, it's a sign that God is carrying away our sins. It's all part of the Rosh Hashanah festival."

"This boy is definitely getting a lesson on Jewish customs this year," put in Mr. Melchior. He looked like he was returning to his friendly self now, trying to get things back to normal. "You don't mind, do you, Peter? We're not trying to convert you from being Lutheran, I hope you know."

"I know," said Peter, and he couldn't help smiling. "I don't mind learning." He really didn't. Then he thought of something.

"What happens if a bird comes and eats all the crumbs?" he blurted out. Mrs. Melchior looked puzzled. Henrik started to giggle. Peter felt almost the same way he did after his "one hundred herring" answer in school.

"No matter," smiled Mr. Melchior between mouthfuls of cabbage. "It's the thought that counts."

10

WAKE-UP CALL

After dinner, Henrik and Peter were in charge of the dishes. Of course, Henrik was drying because of his cast.

"So forget the bird race," said Peter. "We can do other stuff . . . keep racing them around town. It was a stupid idea anyway. We knew your parents didn't want you to get mixed up with my uncle."

"Yeah," Henrik said as he polished a plate extra hard. "Besides, it has been getting pretty scary outside lately."

Both of them thought about the times in the past weeks when they had been close enough to the German soldiers to see reflections in their boots. And while they didn't know too much about the war, they knew that there were German soldiers everywhere, not to mention German trucks, German ships, and German planes. Lately, Peter and Henrik were even scared to send Morse code messages between their windows.

"Hey, since you're here tonight, we don't even have to send a message," said Henrik as they finished up the dishes and moved into the next room. Mrs. Melchior had pulled out a pile of fresh bed sheets, and they rolled them out on the floor next to Henrik's bed.

"That's another thing," said Peter, pulling a corner of the blanket. "I'm not sure if we should be doing that signal-light thing anymore. You know what happened to old Mrs. Bohr last week."

Two nights ago, old Mrs. Bohr down the street had her living room window shot out just because she had forgotten to pull the blackout shade in time. A German soldier had simply aimed at the light. Of course, Mrs. Bohr didn't remember much of anything these days, Peter's mom said. She said the shot had gone through the window, through the living room wall, and all the way through to the next room. Just missed a photo of old Mr. Bohr, who had been dead for twenty-some years. Peter didn't know all the neighbors on their busy street, but when things like this happened, everybody noticed and did what they could.

Henrik didn't say anything for a minute. He was slipping a pillowcase on a pillow, studying it hard. Then he looked up. "I thought about that, too," he said. "Like I said, it's a good thing you're here tonight. So we don't have to." Then he smiled. "Maybe we should get little radios, like the Resistance guys."

Just then Henrik's mother called in from the hallway. "And don't forget what happened to poor old Mrs. Bohr," she said.

"Yes, Mother," Henrik called back. "I mean, no, we won't even think about touching the shades."

With school the next day, the boys had to turn out their lights around nine. Peter had all his books with him, his backpack, a clean shirt, and some underwear. He was still amazed his parents let him spend the night on a Thursday.

After lights were out, the blackout shades made the Melchior living room seem darker than the inside of an icebox at midnight. Henrik and Peter both lay still, neither saying a word for a long time. Peter was in Henrik's bed, and Henrik was down on the floor, comfortable on a thick oval rug.

"Peter, are you awake?"

"What else?" Peter whispered back. Henrik's parents had gone to bed early, too.

"Are you upset that my dad won't let us race the pigeons anymore?"

"He didn't say that exactly," Peter corrected him. "He just didn't want you getting mixed up with my uncle anymore, or getting into too much trouble."

"Isn't that the same thing?"

Peter had to think about that one for a minute. "I'm not sure," he said finally. "I've thought about it lately, and, well, maybe your dad is right."

Henrik didn't say anything for a long time. Peter figured his friend was probably thinking about his father, and about being Jewish. Mr. Melchior seemed to worry too much. On the other hand, there *was* a lot to be worried about.

After a while, Henrik broke the silence. "I don't know, Peter. I can't figure it out. How long do you think this stuff is going to go on?" He was talking about the war, not about pigeons or parents. "I mean, we were nine when it started, weren't we?"

"Eight, I think," said Peter. "Yeah, eight, because it was the month after my eighth birthday that the Germans came. The first year after you moved here."

"So, do you think my dad's right, though? About Danish Jews having to be so careful?"

"I don't know, I don't know, I don't know," Peter whispered. "I'm only eleven, too. And just barely. But my dad says the Germans are starting to lose lots of battles now, and lots of people hope the Americans or the English will come chase them out pretty soon."

"But about the Jews," Henrik whispered.

"All I know is that if anybody ever comes looking for you, you can hide under my bed," Peter said, giving up on the subject. *How am I supposed to know?*

"Not funny." Henrik struggled to stay awake, but his voice was getting farther away, sleepier.

"I didn't mean it like that," Peter said, sorry that he tried to make a joke when Henrik sounded so serious. He wanted to talk more, but in the darkness, he couldn't think of what else to say. *Maybe tomorrow,* he thought, *when we're both more awake.* "Henrik, are you awake?"

This time there was no answer.

As Peter drifted off, he wrestled with his own questions, the same way he had for the past few nights. It seemed like the only time he could really think. But there were too many questions, and they were winning the wrestling match. Danish Jews, or Jewish Danes? Did it matter? Why did the Germans seem to care so much? Never in his life had he heard so much talk about Jews, or about being Jewish, or being in trouble just because you were Jewish. Never, ever—and it was too much for him to figure out at that time of night.

Peter dreamed, and it was something really silly, like soldiers were shooting at his pigeons, and they were flying to Peter to hide. The birds were talking, yelling at him, but he couldn't understand what they were saying because it was a different language.

"Peter! Peter!" He woke up in a sweat; someone was shaking him awake. It was Henrik, leaning over the bed, still in his pajamas. The hallway light was on, and Peter could just see his face. His eyes were wide with fright.

"Peter, wake up!" This was no dream, and Henrik in his pajamas was no talking pigeon.

"Huh?" said Peter, still groggy. "What's going on?" He looked over at Henrik's alarm clock on the dresser. Five-thirty in the morning.

"My dad just woke me up," said Henrik, his voice shaking a little. "He wants us to get dressed right away and get down to the kitchen." Before Peter could complain, Henrik was out the door. So Peter pulled a pair of pants over his pajamas and followed as quickly as he could. Something was very wrong. He shivered, not just from the chill.

Stumbling down the hall and into the kitchen, he recognized the grocery storekeepers from down the street, Mr. and Mrs. Lumby, Ole the mailman, and a man named Albeck. They were all gathered around the Melchior dinner table, where Peter had eaten the holiday dinner just hours before. The expressions on their faces said they weren't having a pleasant cup of morning coffee, though. Especially not at 5:30 A.M.

"I knew it was going to happen," wheezed Mr. Lumby. His round, pink face seemed even pinker, he was so worked up. "I knew it. We couldn't keep pretending we live in some kind of fairyland, that it would never happen here. Look what's already happened to our people in Poland and Austria."

"Okay, Lumby," interrupted Ole. He was small and wiry, with a sharp chin and white, bushy eyebrows. But he was quick with a wave and a smile as he came bouncing down the street with his mail sack. Most of the kids liked him. He seemed different this morning, though—intense or nervous, like everyone else at the table. He was waving his hands and pointing as he spoke. "We know what's happened all over Europe. It doesn't do any good to throw up our hands and say it can't happen here. It can and it has. Me, I'm surprised it didn't happen sooner. Now we have only until tonight—twelve, maybe thirteen hours before the Germans begin their roundup. So we have to act, and we have to act now."

"Well, as soon as I got the phone call from my cousin in Copenhagen, that's when I called you," said Mr. Albeck, looking at Henrik's father, who was also sitting at the table. Then Peter remembered—Mr. Albeck was Henrik's father's brother-in-law. Henrik's uncle. "I was out on a business call, or I would have known earlier. I just wish one of us would have heard a few hours earlier."

"I don't get it," Henrik put in. He had been standing at the kitchen door with Peter. Neither of the boys really knew what everyone was talking about, but they were starting to get the idea that this was some sort of terrible secret they didn't want to know.

Everyone in the room turned to look at them, two kids with rumpled clothes and dumb, sleepy expressions on their faces. Mrs. Lumby and Henrik's mom looked as if they had been crying.

Then Mrs. Melchior looked right at Peter and smiled kindly—the way she had the night before when he was feeling awkward at the dinner table. "Peter, you're welcome to stay for breakfast," she said, "but I think it would be best if you returned home very soon. For your safety. Mr. Melchior has just called your father."

"But, Father, what's going on?" Henrik asked again.

Mr. Melchior took a deep breath, took off his round glasses and carefully began polishing them. "No school today, Henrik, I'm afraid." A quick smile flashed across his face, but it disappeared just as quickly. He was warming up for a little speech. "Well, here in Denmark, it used to be that no one has ever cared that we are Jews, any more than we care if you are left-handed or blue-eyed. The German Nazi soldiers and their leader, Mr. Hitler, on the other hand, have an entirely different opinion, and—"

A soft, quick rap on the front door interrupted Mr. Melchior. Everyone jumped, even Henrik's mom in the kitchen.

"Who could that be?" Mr. Melchior whispered to his wife. "Ruth, would you—no, I'll get it." Henrik's dad pushed out his chair from the kitchen table while everyone looked at one another as if they were wondering what to do. Maybe hide?

In his red robe and slippers Mr. Melchior looked more like he should have been letting the cat out on a Sunday morning. But before anyone could wonder who was out there, Mr. Andersen's muffled voice came through the front door.

"It's Arne Andersen, Mr. Melchior," said Peter's dad, almost as if he were whispering.

Mr. Melchior's stiff back relaxed, and he quickly ran down the stairs to unbolt and open the door. When he came up, Peter's dad stood for a moment at the entrance to the kitchen—only a moment—taking everyone in at a glance. He said good morning to Peter with his eyes.

"Come in, Arne. You're a little early, but the coffee is already hot." Mr. Melchior was getting back some of his humor. "I was just explaining to the boys here what has happened. Have you heard any details?"

Peter's dad nodded quickly. "I've made a couple of calls, and we've confirmed that the Germans are planning their roundup of all Danish Jews for tonight and tomorrow morning. It will happen all over the country at the same time, but of course most of the Jews are in Copenhagen, not here in Helsingor. But the Nazis stole a list with the name of nearly every Jewish family in the country, so they know who you are and where you live."

Mrs. Lumby, the storekeeper's wife, buried her face in her hands and started to cry again, softly.

Peter's father continued. "Now people are deciding whether they will hide and wait, or flee immediately." He shoved his hands into his pockets and scanned the room again. No one else said a word.

"My brother Morten, as you know, is a fisherman, and we can use his boat to get you all over to Sweden immediately if that is what you want. I recommend it. There is no need for waiting. It is clear what is happening."

Mrs. Lumby hadn't said anything since Henrik and Peter had come into the room, but now she stood up, wiped at her eyes with a handkerchief, and looked at Peter's father. "What about our homes, and our businesses?" she said.

That kind of talk went on for thirty minutes or so, while

Henrik and Peter tried to follow it as best they could. It turned out that the Germans planned to round up all Danish Jews on the second evening of Rosh Hashanah: that night, Friday, September 30. The Germans must have figured out that all the Jews would be at home, having another nice dinner. And they probably all would have if a German official who had heard of Hitler's plan hadn't leaked the word the day before to the Danish Jewish leaders. That gave all six or seven thousand Danish Jews less than two days to pack a bag, hide, or get away. Forty-eight hours.

"I had no idea my dad knew all about that stuff," Peter said to Henrik as they returned to Henrik's room. Peter had to get his things before he left with his father.

Henrik pulled his brown canvas school sack from under his bed and dumped his school books with a crash. "It's not fair!" he yelled, picking up one of his school books and throwing it in the corner, hard. Peter winced. "Who says we have to just pick up and leave? What happened to the happy and sweet year?"

Peter remembered the words of the Rosh Hashanah apple-in-honey blessing, too. It was just the night before, but now it seemed like years ago, and he felt like throwing some books around, too. Maybe at a Nazi soldier, if he could find one. But he only stood there with his fists clenched, staring at Henrik stuffing socks and underwear into his school knapsack.

"Peter," Mr. Andersen called down the hall. "We have to go now."

Peter wheeled around, startled. "What about the Melchiors?" he asked. "The Germans are coming tonight."

"They're all staying at our house today and tonight, until your uncle returns from his fishing trip. He should be back tonight or tomorrow morning first thing, and we'll have a way over to Sweden for these people."

Peter looked over at Henrik, who was just standing there by

his open sock drawer. It was decided, then.

"They'll be over later, when they're ready," said Mr. Andersen. "So are the rest of the people downstairs. But right now you and I have to leave."

11

THE MINYAN

Mrs. Andersen had never cooked for so many people before in her life, unless you counted the big family reunion picnic two years earlier at Silkeborg Lake. Now they had a different kind of family reunion; it seemed as if every Jew in Helsingor was in the Andersen living room. Elise counted twenty-three.

Besides Elise, Peter, and their dad, there were the three Melchiors, the two Lumbys, Mrs. Lumby's sister and their seven-year-old niece who lived with them, Ole the mailman (he was a single man), Klaus Albeck, his wife and three teenage daughters (Henrik's cousins). Everyone who had been in the Melchior kitchen that morning, and then some. The Rasmussens from down the street came, too, and they brought along an older woman named Mrs. Clemmensen. People had been coming alone or by twos all day, mostly through the alley and by the side entrance to the building. Mr. Albeck also had an elderly mother and her sister, two aunts and an uncle. Actually, that made twenty-five, if you counted Mrs. Andersen, who was slaving out in the kitchen.

Most everyone had brought a bag or two of food, so that helped. And the ladies were always asking what they could do.

"You can help by relaxing and making yourself as comfortable as you possibly can," Mrs. Andersen would tell them all. She smiled like a hostess at a big party. Actually, she probably didn't mind all the people, but it was by far the strangest, largest gathering Peter and Elise had ever seen in their apartment.

For dinner everyone took plates (somebody had thought ahead and brought a few extras), and found a place to sit wherever they could. The older people sat around the dinner table. Everyone chattered about everything, except what was going to happen the next day. They didn't really know what to do with themselves, but they had to keep their voices down, so the neighbors wouldn't wonder what was going on. Elise and Peter scurried around, trying to fetch all the things their mom needed.

Elise was trotting through the living room with an armload of towels when someone knocked at the door, down at the bottom of the stairs. She gasped, jumped, and dumped all the towels all over the floor. Everyone else froze in midsentence. Peter was getting to hate all the mysterious knocks. But at Mr. Andersen's signal, everyone tiptoed quietly out of the room, bringing their plates with them into the bedrooms. Elise scrambled to pick up her towels.

Then Peter's dad opened the door cautiously, while everyone else tried to hear what was going on.

"Excuse me, Mr. Andersen?" came the soft, scared voice of a man. In the kitchen, Peter looked at his sister, who shrugged. She didn't recognize the voice, either. "I understand you are arranging trips to Sweden for people like us."

"Oh?" said Mr. Andersen. He could be a great actor when he wanted to be. "Why would we be doing something like that? I'm a banker, not a travel planner."

"Please," came the voice, "I believe it was your father ..."

your father Kasper said we could stay here for the evening while we waited for the boat."

"Well, Dad is always the generous one, isn't he, now?" Mr. Andersen's voice changed. "Come in, come in. I hope he's not told the whole neighborhood already. Yes, we're having quite a party here. In fact, it's a jolly sleep over." The door closed, and the new family stepped in. Mr. Andersen directed them upstairs to the living room.

At that, everyone in the back rooms came streaming out, and there were hugs and introductions all around. Some of the people knew the new family. Mr. Andersen put out his hands, making a sign for everyone to be more quiet.

"We're the Christensens," the new man announced after they had taken off their coats. His pudgy pink hands and matching waist made Peter guess he was a baker. Elise smiled at his two small girls, who hid behind their mother's skirt. "We left a suitcase outside in the alley, just in case."

"Well, fetch it, man!" said Mr. Andersen, angry for the first time all day. "Or would you like to announce to every German outside that we're now running a hotel for weary Jews?" The man ran out and snatched his case, embarrassed.

Now with the baker and his wife, along with their two little girls, there were twenty-nine.

Eating was the easy part. Everyone shared a bit with the new family, and it seemed there was plenty to spare. Plenty of potatoes, anyway. The harder part was finding a place for twenty-five extra people to sleep in a three-bedroom apartment. Normally, the Andersens had more room than most people they knew, but it was nowhere near enough for this crowd. Especially with only one bathroom.

"So the living room is the men's dormitory," announced Mr. Andersen, taking charge again. Peter liked the way he was making things happen; it was a side of his dad he had never really seen before. He couldn't remember ever seeing his dad stand so tall and straight, marching all over, making sure everyone kept quiet, keeping things in order. *Not bad,* thought Peter. But then, things would get worse before they got better.

Saturday morning, in fact, was horrible.

"So how do we know your brother is coming?" whined baker Christensen for the third time. Mr. Andersen patiently didn't answer. Everyone was awake, dressed, and cleaned for their last day in Denmark. Not all of them had slept, though, and some people's nerves were showing their edges more than others. After the breakfast dishes were done, Elise kept the Christensen girls occupied to take their minds off what was going on. She had found some cards and Elise taught them a simple matching game on the floor.

"The red three," Elise asked them, a little smile playing on her face. "Do you remember where the red three is?"

One of the little girls, Kirsten, giggled and turned over one of the twenty cards, arranged in a square. It was a black nine. Her sister laughed and pointed to where the red three was hiding. The Lumbys' niece sat nearby on the floor, watching shyly.

On the other side of the room, the Albeck girls were staring out the window. Even though they were Henrik's cousins, they didn't talk to Henrik or to anyone else. They just stared out the window, frowning. Peter didn't know them very well, and they were a couple of years older. He went back to his room to see what Henrik was doing.

Henrik was staring out the window, too. He looked over as Peter came in, but didn't say anything.

"So do you still have to go over to your grandfather's place?" asked Henrik. Mr. and Mrs. Andersen had talked about sending Peter and Elise away for the weekend, until everyone was cleared out of the apartment.

"No, I don't think so," replied Peter. "They were going to, but we promised to help extra. Elise is taking care of those little girls. I'm running around for my mom, fetching things. And after all, you're my best friend."

Henrik didn't say anything but went back to staring out the window. For once, he wasn't smiling, or joking, or even talking much. Peter chattered on, hoping to help Henrik feel a little better. "Good thing it's only a day," he said. "Your cousins look like they're climbing the walls. Maybe we should invite Keld and Jesper over to keep them company."

Henrik just smiled.

Peter quietly left his friend sitting by the window and went back to the living room. There Mrs. Christensen, the baker's wife, was also sitting by a window, nervously peeking out every few minutes. She whispered to the others whenever a German patrol or a soldier marched by on the street. There were a lot out that day.

"Dear, we've been watching them for three years now," her husband finally told her. "They're nothing new."

"We have to be extra careful," she spit back, and her gray eyes flashed. "Every Jew in the country is hiding or running now. We have only a few hours more."

Which reminded Peter—Uncle Morten was due back any time.

"I'll go out and check if he's come in yet," he told Elise, who was still on the floor with the kids, by the door. Really, he just wanted a chance to get out of the house. Without another word, he slipped down the stairs and out the door, and ran down the street toward the harbor. He knew better than to ask Henrik if he wanted to come along, though. This was not a good morning for a Jew to be out for a walk.

The *Anna Marie* wasn't in yet, so Peter slipped into the boathouse to wait.

"Here, Number Two," he called out softly to his pigeon. As usual, Number One was strutting around in front of her, bobbing his head and cooing. Number Three was sticking closer to his

parents. Peter waved his hand at them, and Number One fluttered a few feet to another perch. Then Peter checked their water
dish, threw a few dried peas in their food tray, and sat down
next to the big wire cage to wait.

"Hey, want to go bike riding?" came a voice from behind
him. Henrik popped his smiling face into the shed and slipped
in through the door.

"What in the world are you doing here?" Peter barked at
him. "Your parents didn't let you out, did they?"

"Of course not," he shot back, "but I just had to say goodbye
to good old Number One, and I was tired of feeling depressed
and just staring out the window. It was my last chance. I slipped
out after you left, just for a minute. I'll go right back. No one saw
me."

"You're nuts, Henrik. Totally nuts."

The boys sat by the chicken-wire cage for half an hour, neither saying anything. They just watched the birds dance. Once
in a while a pigeon flew up to its wooden perch on the wall,
higher up in the top corner of the coop. Each time, their fluttering
stirred up a pile of feathers. Henrik took a big gray feather and
tucked it into his pocket for a souvenir.

"Hey, when I come back, Number One will probably be a
great-grandfather, right?"

The chatter and rumble of a fishing boat broke their awkward talk, and they both ran to the dirty little window, the one
that faced out to the harbor and the docks below.

"That's him," said Peter, not saying anything Henrik didn't
already know. They ducked as Uncle Morten got nearer to the
dock, only about twenty feet away.

"You go out," said Henrik, suddenly looking afraid. Obviously, he wasn't as brave as he talked. Peter went out and helped
his uncle tie up and unload a couple of boxes. Uncle Morten
grunted with fatigue as he lifted a box onto the deck and closed
his eyes while running his hand across his beard.

Finally, Peter couldn't stand it anymore. "All the Jews are being rounded up," he whispered. There was no one else nearby, only the usual activity of boats loading and unloading, men working in the distance. No one could hear a word they were saying. "Our house is full of them, all waiting for you to take them over to Sweden. Dad said you had already talked about what to do if something like this would happen."

"And so it finally did," said Uncle Morten, shaking his head as if to clear the cobwebs from his mind. His eyes seemed to darken, and he looked around the docks. "We knew it would happen; we just didn't know when." He jerked on a mooring line. "I should have been here. Come on, Peter." Then he looked at the boathouse. "You too, Henrik."

Back at the apartment, Henrik got a thorough scolding from his parents for slipping out, but Uncle Morten's arrival cut things short. There wasn't much time to plan the escape before that night; Uncle Morten, Mr. Andersen, and a few of the other men sat around the kitchen table, talking in low tones.

"That's the best we can figure it," said Peter's father as he pushed back his chair. It was now the middle of the afternoon and lunch dishes were still stacked all over the table.

"I think so, too, big brother," said Uncle Morten. He was only a year or two younger than Peter's father, but the wind and sun had made a difference on the fisherman's face and hands. And Peter's dad, the banker, didn't get as much exercise. Both were pretty rugged looking, though, and there was no doubt they were brothers. Everyone in the room looked up to the two of them, the captain and the banker.

Discussion over, Uncle Morten tapped his drinking glass with a spoon, signaling a speech. Everyone hushed, even the little kids.

"Before we start our trip tonight," he said, "I'd like to offer a word of prayer." Everyone just stared at him, not sure what to say. It was quiet. Very quiet. Uncle Morten looked around for a brief second, judging their expressions.

"I know we don't share exactly the same beliefs," he said finally. "But, um, we started out in the same place. My Bible and your Torah, the books of Moses, both talk about the same Abraham, Isaac, and Jacob. So I'd like to pray for you anyway."

Both Mr. Melchior and Peter's dad looked at Uncle Morten, then at each other. Henrik's father broke the ice with his famous smile. It was easy to tell where Henrik got his from.

"At least we have a minyan now, right?" said Mr. Melchior. A couple of the men chuckled. He sounded as if he were explaining the Jewish feast, back at his own home. He looked over at Peter and winked. "A minyan, non-Jewish friends, is the number of men we need for a Jewish worship service. Ten. Yes, by all means, we should pray." He looked back at Uncle Morten and nodded. "So pray."

The big fisherman bowed his head then and stuffed his hands into his pockets. Peter had to peek at what was going on, and he caught Elise's eye. She looked like she didn't quite know what to make of the praying uncle and the houseful of Jews either, and she glanced quizzically at Peter as if he could explain the whole thing with just a look. Some of the others in the house still looked surprised, but they too bowed their heads.

"Lord God," began Uncle Morten. With his head bowed and his eyes squinting, Peter could just imagine how the voice would sound in a Jewish synagogue. "You have brought your people to this place for a reason, and it is no mistake. Tonight we bow before you as King, asking that you would bring them, once again, safely out of the danger they face. Please make for them a way through the sea, to safety, as if it were the Red Sea." He paused, looking for a word. "And bring them home again soon. . . ."

"Amen," said more than one voice.

When Peter opened his eyes, he saw most of the people were sniffling, or crying, or both. He looked over at Elise, who was standing by the kitchen door, dabbing at her eyes. His uncle's prayer made him think about where all these people would go, and he wondered if they would really come back. He knew that pretty soon he would be crying too, so he slipped down the hall to the bathroom.

CONVOY

Mr. Andersen was in charge of the land part of the escape, Uncle Morten the sea part. As Mrs. Andersen began to turn on dim lights around the house, he explained the plan one more time.

"Now, all of you listen, please," said Mr. Andersen, almost like a first-grade schoolteacher introducing the alphabet. "I've explained it to everyone several times, but I want to make completely sure everyone knows exactly what's happening." Peter looked around the room. Even though everyone had heard it all before, even two times, no one dared take their eyes away from his dad.

"Now, who's riding in the first truck—the mail van?" The Christensens, the mailman, and the older Albeck relatives raised their hands. "The ambulance follows by fifteen minutes. Who is on that?" Mr. Andersen looked around the room, nodding intensely at the people as they raised their hands. That group included Henrik and his parents, plus Mr. Albeck, his wife and three daughters. Mrs. Clemmensen, too. She didn't seem to hear very much and nodded at all the wrong times. Peter felt himself admiring his father again, in a strange, new way. *Maybe Dad should have been a teacher after all, the way he handles this group.*

"And the last car we could scrape up—the old Mercedes— who is riding in that one?" Five people raised their hands. One of the little Christensen girls, who was about six, thought this part was pretty exciting. "I want to ride in the trunk!" she announced. Elise, who was holding her hand, smiled down at her. Any other time, everyone would have laughed. Now, there were only a few chuckles.

"That's no joke," said Mr. Andersen. "One of you *will* be riding first class, I mean in the trunk. We'll load in the alley. I will be driving the first car, and it will be up to the driver of each vehicle to keep order. There will of course be no talking, no sounds, and no delays. None whatsoever. We will all load the boat in the same order. And remember . . ." His voice got a little more serious. "There will be no need for excuses if anyone is caught. The Germans will know exactly who you are and what you are trying to do." He looked around the room at all the eyes—old eyes, scared eyes, and petrified little eyes. Everyone knew exactly what he was saying, except for the youngest ones.

"However, if they insist on knowing where you gathered and who helped you, it would be best if you all have the same story. My family and I want to continue living in Denmark, without major trouble from the Germans, if that is possible. So our story is this: You were all assisted by Joachim Etlar, and you gathered at his house. He is a good Jew. Do you understand?"

There were a lot of blank stares, until the baker squinted his eyes and looked at Uncle Morten, who was sitting next to his brother. "Pardon me," said the pudgy little man, "but I've not seen Mr. Etlar for several days. He always used to come into my bakery for his morning bread, but not lately."

Uncle Morten smiled slightly, almost nervously. "You are

right, Mr. Christensen. Etlar will not be coming home for quite a while, either. Please believe me."

"Does everyone understand that now?" asked Mr. Andersen. All the adults nodded. Peter hoped no one would ask any more questions. Peter didn't want to know about Mr. Etlar, either—whether he had really been a good man and escaped somehow, or if he had gotten mixed up on the wrong side of the Danish Resistance movement. They had heard about what happened to the few people who decided to help the Germans.

"Good," continued Mr. Andersen, waving his hand at his brother. "Please remember that my good brother Morten will bring the boat around to a quiet beach just up the coast. The drivers know the spot. We will wait there in the darkness, and there is a small boat available at a summer beach house there. Again, we will ferry out to the boat in the same order we got into the cars. Completely silent. Not a sneeze out of anyone, and that includes the children. Parents, please make sure of that. Now the boat, the *Anna Marie*, will be a bit cramped, but everyone should fit into the fishhold just fine." Then he looked at Uncle Morten. "Right, Morten?"

"No problem," said Uncle Morten. "The only thing is, I didn't have time to clean it out very thoroughly after we got back. So I'm afraid that when you get to Sweden, you'll be smelling like a fine catch of pickled herring."

Everyone looked at one another, afraid to smile, afraid to move. Mr. Andersen looked around the room. Old Mrs. Clemmensen started knitting her fingers together nervously.

"Let's take the last couple of hours getting all our things together," he said. "If you have any questions about what is going to happen, please ask me or Morten."

As late afternoon turned toward evening, Uncle Morten slipped out to get his boat ready. It was almost time for the caravan to leave. After a few phone calls, Mr. Andersen left to get the mail van.

Even though they had cleaned up from the last meal several hours before, Peter found his mother in the kitchen, still clanging pots. Elise had taken a break from her constant baby-sitting and was helping her mother put things away.

"Mom?" said Elise, opening up a cupboard. Mrs. Andersen gave her daughter a smile.

"Are Dad and Uncle Morten going to be okay ... I mean, what would happen to them if ..." She lowered her voice, making sure no one in the next room could hear them.

"Don't you worry about them for a minute, Elise," said Mrs. Andersen, putting her arm around her daughter's shoulder. She reached for Peter, also, who gladly accepted a hug from his mother. "Your praying uncle and your smart daddy are going to be just fine."

Peter wanted to believe her, but he couldn't stop worrying. What if? By the look on his sister's face, she couldn't either. No one wanted to think about it. Mother, daughter, and son didn't say anything else but pretended to find something to do, scrubbing the stove, polishing the sink.

Ten minutes later, Ole the mailman came tiptoeing in from the bathroom, where he had been keeping watch out the small window.

"The mail van is here," he croaked.

13

On the Run

Everyone looked at one another, and a few of them shook hands. There wasn't time for much else. Then the first small group assembled by the door, silent now.

"Remember, through the courtyard and out the side alley entrance," whispered Mrs. Andersen as she released the first load of Jews, one at a time, through the door. At the bottom of the stairs, a side door opened into the small, dark courtyard, closed in by buildings. Another door led out to the side alley, where the getaway cars would be parked, one at a time, in the shadows. It took almost twenty minutes to filter them through, a little longer than planned, so they were already behind schedule. Then they were gone, Mr. Andersen at the wheel of the mail truck. This was a special delivery.

Loading the next car—the ambulance—went more quickly, until Mrs. Clemmensen started crying. She was alone and she grabbed hold of Mrs. Andersen the way some little kids do the first morning of kindergarten. Peter, who was sitting in the living room, had seen that kind of panic before. She was not going to let go.

"We must load the ambulance quickly," urged Mr. Melchior, who was now in charge of the second group. He was trying to get Mrs. Clemmensen to move into the hallway. That only made the old woman hold on even more tightly, which was kind of odd because they had never met before yesterday. People were starting to panic. "Come on!" whispered Mrs. Lumby from the stairs, a bit impatiently. The old woman was now sobbing, and Mrs. Andersen was trying to calm her. But she would not be comforted.

Mr. Melchior looked around nervously, then looked at Peter's mother. "I hate to ask you," he said, "but will you go with Mrs. Clemmensen in the ambulance? We need to go, and now."

Mrs. Andersen only hesitated for a moment, then nodded. By now, almost everyone else had loaded into the ambulance, including Henrik's mother. The only ones left were Mr. Melchior, who was going to drive, Henrik, and old Mrs. Clemmensen.

"Go with her, then, Mrs. Andersen," said Mr. Melchior as he urged the panicked woman and Peter's mother through the door. They almost looked like Siamese twins.

"But that was the last place," said Mrs. Andersen, looking at Henrik. There wasn't even time for her to tell Peter and Elise what to do. She looked over her shoulder with a worried expression on her face. Peter got up from the couch, and Elise came and stood next to him.

"You just lock the door and stay in the apartment after everyone is gone," she commanded. "Don't open up for anyone until your father and I get back, do you understand? And Elise, you take care of your brother. I'll ride back with Dad. We'll be back in no more than a couple of hours."

They both nodded seriously as she left with the terrified Mrs. Clemmensen wrapped around her like a pretzel. Peter wondered how his mother would ever untangle herself.

Mrs. Clemmensen wasn't the last crisis Henrik's dad had to deal with, though. He bit his lip, then turned to his son with a worried expression. "That means you'll have to go in the third car, Henrik." He looked around for Mr. Lumby, who was in charge of the third group, but the storekeeper must have been outside, parking the last car. Henrik's dad had to leave or the whole schedule would fall apart. He looked around, trying to decide.

"Okay," he finally said to Henrik. "You go with the third car. But be sure to tell Lumby exactly what happened now, will you?" He waved his finger in Henrik's face for effect. "Your mother will be furious that you don't get in the second car with us. But now there is nothing to do about it. If we can, we'll stop at the corner to make sure you get going all right."

Henrik nodded seriously. "I'll tell him, Father. There's room in the trunk. Go ahead. We'll be fine."

Mr. Melchior started through the door, the last one out for that group. Peter and Elise stood there with Henrik. Mr. Melchior stopped for a moment, then turned around to look at his son. Henrik tried to make him feel better. "It's no problem, Father. Really. I'm eleven, remember?"

Mr. Melchior nodded, though he didn't look encouraged. With a pat on his son's shoulder, he was gone.

In a few more minutes it was time to load the third car, and Mr. Lumby finally appeared. The first two had taken a little longer than anyone expected. It was getting dark by then, and German patrols of two or three soldiers were starting to come down the street often enough to be a threat. This had to happen fast.

Peter turned out all the lights in the apartment, and Elise kept watch from his bedroom window. Even though their mother had given them firm instructions to stay put until they got back, they could still help. So Peter went back and forth between the hallway and the living room, relaying information from Elise. Mr.

Lumby, the leader of the third group, checked with Peter. He looked nervously out of each window, too, then waved the first people out.

Henrik's turn was next. "We kind of already said goodbye in the pigeon coop," he said to Peter as he stood near the doorway.

"Yeah, but I'm still going to miss you," Peter added. His stomach felt like a knot.

"See you when we get back," Henrik whispered. He gave Peter a quick hug, stopped at the bedroom door for a second to say goodbye to Elise, and then ran down the stairs to the side door.

"Go!" said Mr. Lumby. And Henrik was gone.

Next went Mr. and Mrs. Rasmussen, and Mr. Lumby was getting more and more nervous. He always had been a little edgy to begin with.

Suddenly Elise appeared in the doorway, waving frantically at Peter. "Nazi coming!"

Peter ran to the stairway just as Mr. Lumby was sending out the next couple. "No, wait!" Peter whispered as loud as he dared.

"What?" It took only a second for Mr. Lumby to realize what was going on. He yanked the frightened couple back into the courtyard. They had hardly put a foot out the door. Everyone held their breath as the soldier strolled by. All of them waited for what seemed like forever; it must have been three minutes.

"Okay, clear," Elise called more softly when the soldier had strolled out of sight, and Mr. Lumby sent the Rasmussens out to hide in the car. The last car was parked far back in the alley, mostly out of sight behind a lineup of street poles and large garbage cans. Mr. Lumby, Peter, and Elise retreated for a minute up to the bedroom window to get a better view of what was going on.

Now there was someone else out on the street, wandering

from the same direction the soldier had first come. He went up to a door, checked the address number, then went to the next one. The dark figure came up to the front entrance of the Andersens' building, almost directly underneath Peter's window. He stopped, then looked up at the dark window. Mr. Lumby sucked in his breath.

"That's Abrahamsen," he said, whistling under his breath. "What's a Jew doing out on the street on a night like this?" Considering what they were doing, Peter thought that was an obvious question. Peter started down the hall, but Mr. Lumby ran past him and down the stairs. He had the front street door open almost before the first light knock. From the top of the stairs, Peter could hear the two men whispering fiercely.

"Yes, there's probably room for one more," came Mr. Lumby's voice. "But . . ."

"Look, I can pay for passage on the boat, too." The other man sounded desperate. "I know it's expensive, but I heard the boat was leaving tonight, and . . ."

That went on for a few intense moments, and Peter returned to the bedroom to keep watch with his sister. The two men must have moved to the courtyard; for a moment, Peter couldn't hear their voices anymore. They would have to hurry and decide what they were going to do with this extra man.

In the meantime, the side door opened, and Henrik came quietly up the stairs from the alley and the courtyard. Peter was too surprised at seeing Henrik again in the apartment to say anything.

"I have to . . ." Henrik mumbled as he raced into the small bathroom down the hall. "Couldn't wait until we got to Sweden. We still have a minute until everyone is loaded."

"But, Henrik—" Peter started to whisper as Henrik slammed the door in his face. "Henrik, hurry!" He was thinking about the extra passenger and the nervous Mr. Lumby.

"No worry," Henrik called from the washroom. "I'll be out in just a second."

A second turned into a long minute until Henrik was out again. Elise poked her head out of Peter's room.

"What's going on?" she asked.

"That's what I want to know," said Peter. They all ran down the side stairs, expecting Mr. Lumby and Mr. Abrahamsen at the door. No one was there.

"No!" cried Henrik. He ran as fast as he could past the garbage cans in the dark courtyard and up to the side alley door.

Elise and Peter didn't know what Henrik was doing, but they knew he couldn't go running out into the street, making a scene. There were still too many soldiers strolling around. They both sprinted after him.

"Henrik!" whispered Elise. "You can't go out there!"

He hesitated for just a moment at the door, which gave Peter and Elise a precious second to catch up. Of course, Henrik could outrun both of them, broken arm or no broken arm.

"I'm leaving," he called from the doorway. They were three steps away.

As Henrik opened the door to run out, Peter jumped at the doorknob as it started to open, and Elise grabbed Henrik's shoulders.

"No! I have to go!" Henrik yelled. *There had better not be any soldiers out there right now,* thought Peter, *or they'll hear us for sure.*

"You can't, Henrik," said Elise. "Let's look out there first."

Peter was having a tug-of-war with the door and Henrik, and even though Henrik was tugging, he was starting to give up against his two friends.

"You run out there now," said Peter, "and you might as well turn yourself in to the Germans."

Henrik looked straight at Peter, and his eyes looked wild. Peter still held on to him, then Elise carefully, quietly, peeked out.

"It's gone," she whispered.

Henrik didn't say anything but looked out himself. Finally, he let Peter gently pull him back from the doorway. Then he turned around, groaned, and sank to his knees. "How could they have left without me? How? I promised my dad I would leave on time with the third car, and they just drove off without me!" His shoulders shook, and Elise and Peter held on to him once more. They let him cry.

"That's what I was trying to tell you," said Peter, explaining how the last passenger had shown up unexpectedly at the door. "I guess Mr. Lumby must have told him he could come along. I thought for sure they saw you come back into the house, but they must not have, so he probably thought you were still . . ."

"Still in the trunk of the car." Henrik finished the sentence. He was sniffling now as they walked back up the stairs. "I closed it after me real quietly so no one would see a car sitting out there in the alley with its trunk open. And the people waiting in the car were all hunched down, so no one would see them either."

The three of them just looked at one another. No one had a clue what to do next.

"It's my fault," said Peter. "I should have told Lumby right away."

"No, it's not your fault," said Henrik, holding on to Peter's shoulder. "It was my fault for coming back in. It all happened so fast, and Lumby didn't even say goodbye or anything."

"Well, while you boys are trying to figure out who to blame, let's go up to the window to see if we can still see them," Elise finally suggested. "Maybe someone will notice you're gone, and they'll come back for you."

Henrik frowned. "I'd rather run after them."

"We'll figure something out," said Elise.

Peter didn't say anything else. But he kept expecting a soldier to come busting through the door any minute after the scene they had made, and after all the noise and yelling. *We could have given away a whole carload of people if we had started running down the street after them.*

But nothing happened, so they went back to Peter's bedroom window. From there, they could see down the street, almost five blocks to Star Street. Two blocks down was the large old Mercedes Benz, the one with the trunk Henrik was supposed to be in, but it wasn't moving. They all strained their eyes in the half-light to see three German soldiers, with rifles drawn, surrounding the car. As the three friends stared, horrified, two of the soldiers grabbed a door and yanked it open. In a moment, people were spilling out into the street: two from the front, four more who had been hiding in the back. No one, of course, came out of the trunk, which didn't surprise anyone looking from Peter's room, but Mr. Lumby was probably mystified. Before long, everyone had been hauled up and lined against the car by the gun-pointing soldiers, even the Lumbys' young niece.

Elise turned away from the window. "Even the little girl," she whispered in shock.

All Peter heard for the longest time was the ticking of the wall clock out in the living room. None of them could cry.

Finally, Elise looked at Henrik. "Listen, Henrik, I know what you're thinking, and it wasn't your fault."

"How do you know? Didn't the soldiers just come out of the shadows and stop the car? Maybe they heard us."

"That's silly," said Peter. "If anybody had heard us, we wouldn't still be here." He wasn't so sure, but that sounded right to him. Peter was afraid to look out the window anymore, afraid to see something else horrible happen. But in a few more minutes he did, and the car was still there, pulled to the curb. No one else was in sight, though—no Danes, no Jews, no German soldiers. Peter's stomach felt tight and his hands sweaty. *Maybe the soldiers are waiting for more people to drive down the street, and they'll just step out of the shadows . . .*

"This isn't turning out to be much of a rescue for you," Peter finally said to Henrik, who by now was just sitting on the floor with his head in his hands.

Elise didn't say a word but sat on the bed, staring vacantly across the room. Suddenly her eyes lit up. "Hey, wait a minute," she said. "Maybe there's a chance Uncle Morten hasn't left the harbor yet. It's just about dark now, and if we keep to the alleys, and stay behind things and look out for anybody coming, we can probably make it down to the harbor without the Germans bothering us."

"Well, I don't know," said Henrik.

"Come on," she said, bravely now. "We're just three kids, remember? One with a broken arm even. What would they care? You have any better ideas?"

Peter wasn't so sure either, but if there was a chance that his uncle was still around . . .

Henrik looked like he was thinking it over. Then he stood up.

"Okay," he said, sounding more sure of himself. "But only if you stay here, Elise. I don't want you getting into more trouble for me. It would only be—"

"Absolutely not!" said Elise, the color rising in her face. She sounded the same way she did when she was in the school auditorium that day, scolding the local bullies. "First of all, it was my idea. And second of all, I'm not staying here alone!"

"But your mom told you two to stay here, didn't she?" Henrik was giving it one last try, but he was going to lose this argument.

"Just like your dad told you to get in the last car, right?" Peter said. "We're going with you, and that's that. Besides, we'll be back way before anyone else."

Just in case their mom or dad got home before they did, though, Peter scribbled a note and left it on the kitchen table: "Mom/Dad: Elise and I had to go with Henrik down to the boat to catch Uncle Morten. Henrik missed the car. Back soon. Sorry, emergency! P & E."

Peter knew they would have a lot of explaining to do when they got home, especially if his parents got home before they did. But yes, this was a life-or-death emergency if he ever saw one. *What choice do we have? We have to get Henrik down to the boat.* Still, he was afraid his loudly beating heart would give them away as they crouched in the alley.

Peter put his head down to the street before looking out around the corner of the building. It was a trick he'd read about in his Boy Scout handbook on tracking animals. "If you put your head way down to the forest floor before looking out behind a tree," he whispered, "the animal will be less likely to notice you."

"What animal are you talking about?" Elise whispered back. He just shook his head.

They decided that if anyone chased them, they would lead the chaser on for a minute, then split directions, and then meet at the boathouse. All Peter could think of as they tiptoed out across the street was the picture of that carload of Jews, stopped and dragged out like animals. Henrik looked down the street in the direction of where it happened.

"I'm glad you weren't in the trunk," Peter whispered at Henrik.

"Shh . . ."

They paused at the next corner, avoiding the busier streets, even though there was hardly anyone out at this time. When it got close to being dark, people in Helsingor pretty much stayed inside, especially lately. Peter looked up at the second-floor windows, all of them dark with blackout blinds. Everyone else was probably sitting in their living rooms, reading a book or something. *So what are we doing out here?*

Down Stone Street, Peter could see a few dim lights coming out of a pub. Local people mostly stayed away from it because it had become a hangout for German soldiers. If they didn't go past it, though, they would lose precious time going all the way around the block.

"Come on!" Henrik surprised Peter and Elise by ungluing his feet first. They all knew the way. As they shuffled closer, Peter tried to melt into the sides of the buildings and shops. Olsen's Bakery. He and Elise took turns fetching their fresh morning bread there, even though their dad grumbled that there weren't any pastries anymore, not since the war had started. Kastrup's Women's Clothing. Mrs. Andersen was getting to be an expert at mending things lately, and nowadays she only stopped at the window for a quick look. Stone Street Apotek—the pharmacy. Mr. Andersen was good friends with Mr. Parslov, the pharmacist. Elise and Peter had to run down there to pick up medicine for their mom every once in a while. Now the German pub was only two doors away, and Peter could almost feel the eyes, looking out the door, looking for Henrik.

Even though it was on the opposite side of the street, they could hear the Germans laughing and chattering as if they were in the same room with them. Peter couldn't understand much— just a word here and there—which was probably a good thing.

Just then the pub door banged open hard, and a young soldier marched out into the middle of the deserted street. Peter looked over. *Not again!* Like a flock of birds changing direction all at once, the three of them ducked into a door well, a little covered doorway spot in front of the pharmacy, and hugged the shadows tightly.

It was dark in the entry, but there were a few small nightlights on inside the store. Their light just made it out to the street. Right about then, Peter was wishing he could trade spots with his pigeon. Any pigeon. *I'd settle for being that size right now.*

For what seemed like forever, they froze like mannequins in the dark doorway. During that same forever the soldier crossed the street, paused and sniffed, looked both directions, then bent over and held his knees. The soldier was only a few feet away now. He looked through his pockets for something, then he teetered a little as he brought out a cigarette and tried to light it. It took him three matches to find his mouth, and Peter was surprised he didn't burn his nose.

Peter could feel Henrik's ankle twitching like crazy, and he knew his friend had stopped breathing a long time ago. Elise was behind them, silent. Peter didn't dare look. *Leave, leave, leave—Go away!* Finally the soldier got his cigarette lighted, then followed the orange glow uncertainly out into the middle of the street. If he turned just a little to the right, he would be staring straight at the three mannequins in the doorway. He took another step closer.

"Run!" Henrik grabbed Peter's shoulder, trying to drag him out of the doorway, and started sprinting down the street. Peter grabbed Elise's hand. Then he took one look at the surprised, drunk soldier and forced his feet to move.

"Can't chat, sorry," Henrik called back as they ran down the street past the startled soldier. "Past my bedtime."

If the man was going to shoot, thought Peter, he wouldn't be able to hit the side of City Hall, even if he were standing next to it. *Crazy Henrik.*

Peter forced his legs to move faster and faster, and Elise seemed to match him footstep for footstep. All they heard was the pounding of their feet and the soggy soldier cursing in the darkness behind them. They were too scared to split up as they had planned. Two blocks later, Henrik slowed to a trot and looked over his shoulder. Elise and Peter puffed up behind him.

"One down, how many to go?" he asked as they stopped in another dark entryway.

"No joke, Henrik," puffed Peter. "That was pretty close." In the back of his mind, it seemed to Peter that they had once had the same conversation. They kept walking, even more carefully now, and he remembered the close call with the lost German soldier at the hotel. But there was no more time to think back. Two more blocks of shadow-to-shadow walking, and they made it to the harbor.

"I hope he's still here," Elise said quietly.

The first thing they saw was the boathouse, and of course there was no light on inside. Below the shack the walkway sloped down to a floating dock, which by now—at low tide— was way down. This was the same spot where Henrik had broken his arm just a few days ago. Would the boat still be there? Elise was the first one there, but she just stopped at the top of the ramp, saying nothing.

"Well," Henrik said finally, looking out at the empty dock where the boat should have been. "I guess we ran all the way over here for nothing."

"Did you have any better ideas?" Peter thought he had asked that question already. But now they were really out of ideas. They stood there, and Peter wished there could have been some kind of mistake, and the boat would suddenly reappear.

It was Elise who finally broke the silence. "Let's not stand out here," she whispered. "Someone is going to come along."

"Right," Peter agreed. "Let's go in the shed to think for a minute."

Henrik startled the pigeons a little when he walked in; they had already roosted for the night. The faded light from the moon, a tiny little moon, slipped in behind Peter as he and Elise tripped in through the door. For a second, Peter saw Number One. The bird moved his head and stared at them, as if he was upset at the intrusion. But that was it. Once pigeons decide to go to bed, nothing gets them very excited.

Peter and Elise sat down on two dusty stools next to the coop, not daring to turn on the light. The pigeons didn't move a feather. Henrik kicked something in the dark and grunted. Gradually, their eyes got used to the shadows inside. A little bit of light got in through the cracks in the siding, even through the single, dirty little window. On the other side of the small shed, several projects were piled high around the workbench. There were a couple of oars, half varnished, rolls of net and twine, stacks of boards, buckets of paint.

Peter couldn't quite see it, but he knew that on the wooden floor there was still a big paint splotch, a reminder of the time Henrik had dumped paint on his head while they were painting the little—rowboat. *What an idea!*

He tiptoed over to the pile of nets his uncle had thrown over the little yellow boat, and felt his way through the tangle.

Elise followed, pulling off nets from the other side of the pile. "Are you thinking what I'm thinking?" she asked.

Peter couldn't tell her expression in the mostly dark shed, but he suspected she was frowning. "I think so," said her brother.

They were two very different people, but there were those rare times when their minds seemed to work in exactly the same way. This was one of those times.

"Assuming we could get this thing out of here without being seen . . ."

"Which is highly unlikely," she put in.

"And assuming then that we could just row right out of the harbor, right under the noses of the German guards," he said.

"Which also is unlikely."

"Then we'd have to row straight across the Sound," continued Peter.

"Which is pretty far," said his sister.

"Then keep heading for the lights . . ."

"Two miles away."

"And keep this thing floating all the way over," finished Peter.

Henrik had been listening, but now he spoke up. "It was leaking pretty bad the last time we had it out in the harbor," he said, sounding very worried about the idea.

"But we might just make it," said Peter. "Does anybody have any better ideas?"

"Well, yeah, wait a minute," said Elise. "Remember the note we left for Mom and Dad only said we were going down to catch Uncle Morten. They're going to flip when they read the note as it is."

Peter knew. And his parents would know at the beach—right about then—that something had gone wrong.

"Well, what if we just try to get back to the apartment?" asked Henrik. "We could get caught, right?"

That was bad enough trouble for Peter and Elise, but unthinkable for Henrik. Now all three had seen Jews being caught and rounded up. It was getting more and more impossible to just walk around, especially at night.

"This is crazy," Peter said for all of them. They stood still for a moment to think some more. Peter thought of the little boat he and Henrik had worked on and the "Dead Lily" paint. *It just might work.*

"But I think we have a chance at making it over," Peter said again after a minute.

"Yeah, if it were a calm, sunny day, and there were no German patrol boats out there ready to grab us," grumbled Henrik, who had not warmed up to this idea yet.

Peter thought of his parents again. Then he saw the picture in his mind once more, replaying the terrible scene of the Jews in the car, being stopped, pulled out, lined up.

"But hey," he added, "what else can we do?" Now that he had thought it through a little, he tried to sound like it was going to be no big deal.

"I don't know, Peter," Henrik said, his voice quivering. "My parents will think I was captured for sure in that car. Do you think they would have come back for me?"

"And just who do you think they would have explained it to, huh?" asked Peter. "They're Jewish, remember?"

As soon as he said that, Peter bit his tongue. "I'm sorry, Henrik," said Peter, feeling awful. "I didn't mean for it to come out like that. I just meant that—"

"That's okay," said Henrik, sounding like he was trying hard not to cry. "It's true."

"Look," said Elise. "Maybe they figured that the only thing they could do would be to escape the way they planned and hope that my dad or someone could do something to get you back. The only thing I know is that we can't go back to the apartment now. We just need to get you out of here somehow."

Peter thought hard. *Maybe she's wrong for once.* But then he sighed. *Not likely. Not Elise.* "Or how about this?" he suggested. "If we hide here, my uncle could come back and take Henrik over with the next bunch of Jews."

"Maybe," said Henrik. "But I think the only thing for me to do now is row over alone. You guys shouldn't get in trouble, too."

They were quiet for a minute while Elise kept watch out the window.

"Henrik," said Elise, glancing over in the darkness, "think about what you just said."

"Huh? What do you mean?" he asked.

Peter reached over and knocked on his cast.

"Oh, yeah," said Henrik.

Just then Elise tugged at her brother's shoulder. Peter was about to protest, but Elise cut him short.

"Shhh! Look!" she whispered.

Peter crowded over to look out the little window with her, and Henrik looked over his shoulder. Across the shipyard, some big ships that were being fixed sat next to a couple of warehouses with cranes. Here and there, fishing boats and workboats had been hauled out of the water and propped up. During the daytime, Peter loved this place. It smelled like workboats, salt water, and tarred rope. Now it was a shadowy forest of shapes—ship masts and big buildings kept dark because of the blackouts. And two buildings away, a dark figure was checking doors and windows.

He had a large flashlight and kept it off most of the time. Elise had silently pointed him out, though, as he flashed the light into windows and behind buildings. They all watched him enter a small work shed, shine the light around, and try the next one. The security guard.

"This is it," Peter whispered. "We've got to get the boat in the water and get out of here before he sees us."

"Right," agreed Henrik. "If he catches us in here, it's all over." The decision was made for them. They would row. Or at least, Elise and Peter would row. Henrik, with his one arm, would ride.

They ripped the netting off the boat in an instant and threw it into a corner. Next Elise took the pointed front end, and Peter reached over for the back end. With Henrik in the middle, using one arm, they slid the little boat away from the wall, upside down, and Peter tried to lift it off the floor. The railing slipped through his fingers, and the edge of the boat crashed against his toes.

He screamed silently, and they all stood still, waiting for the security guard to come running through the door. Peter felt as if this were a replay of the scene back at the apartment, when the soldiers were walking past their door and they were making all kinds of noises. His toe throbbed.

Nothing happened, though, so they got another grip. This time, Elise and Peter both had a good handle on the boat, and they started for the door. They put the boat down for just a moment while Henrik peeked outside.

All clear.

As they started out the door, with Henrik and Elise in front, Peter remembered how low the tide had been, and how steep the ramp down to the deck was. Backing up, Elise didn't. Just as she was about to go over backwards down the ramp, Peter yanked back hard on his end of the boat. Even in the dim light he could see her frightened expression as she almost fell forward.

"Watch where you're going," whispered Peter. The moon just barely shone on the water far below. Henrik was already down on the dock. Then Elise's eyes got wide as she spotted something behind Peter.

"The guard," Elise hissed. It was Peter's turn to look over his shoulder, and he saw the faint glow of the man's flashlight bobbing around the corner. *We have to go now, even if this ramp looks like Mt. Everest to me.* With a desperate push they both half slid, half tiptoed down the steep ramp. Peter held his breath and gritted his teeth, not sure if the guard had seen them duck down or if he had heard their racket. *After all this . . .*

Somehow they reached the bottom and turned the corner. From there it was easier to flip the little boat over right side up and slide it quietly into the black water of the harbor, in between the bigger fishing boats rafted up on the pier. In their panic, they didn't tie up their little boat but crouched in the darkness on the clammy dock, behind one of the bigger boats.

"Do you think we can slip out now?" whispered Peter.

"Sure, if you want to use your big hands to paddle us across to Sweden," said Henrik.

Peter wanted to hit himself in the head. *I'm so stupid. I didn't even think about the oars.* One of them would have to go back up to the shed for them.

"I'll go," said Henrik. "Back in a second. The guard is probably done checking the shed by now."

Yes, he had, and he was stomping down the gangway to the docks where they were now hiding.

All Peter could think of was to crawl up on the deck of one of the larger fishing boats, and he signaled Elise to follow him. They rolled up in the same motion and crawled on their stomachs behind the wheelhouse, as far opposite from the security guard as they could get. Henrik ducked behind another boat, and Peter wondered how Henrik got around so well with only one good arm. They were holding their breath again, one more time in this cat-and-mouse routine.

The guard took his time coming down the steep ramp, but they were afraid to peek. Peter could just imagine him shining the light full on his face. *What would I say?* The guard shuffled over to where they had left the little rowboat, muttering something in Danish they could barely understand. At least it wasn't in German, Peter thought gratefully, although it didn't really seem to matter at that point.

"Lazy fishermen," came the grumble. It sounded like an older man. There was a pause. "Don't know . . . why I bother." Now they could hear him better. "I should just leave these boats where they sit, let them bang up against all the other boats. Leave 'em untied. Leave all the doors unlocked. They should deal with the mess."

The old security guard mumbled some more to himself as he tied up the small boat to the pier. Then he shuffled back up the dock, flashing his light around the boats. "These people don't know all the extra trouble I . . ." The man's voice trailed off as he again climbed up the ramp and headed back across the boatyard.

Only when they hadn't heard his voice for five minutes did anybody move, or look.

"Is he gone?" Peter asked Elise.

Henrik uncurled from his spot behind a packing crate. "Yeah, he won't be back now," he said.

"You sound sure of yourself," said Peter. He looked around, too. Maybe Henrik was right, but it was too dark to tell. And he was feeling again like he really wanted to be back home, or at least anywhere other than here. He thought once more about getting the oars, but Henrik was already going up after them.

"Henrik!" whispered Elise. "Stay here. We'll get the oars!"

But Henrik acted as if he couldn't hear. From the top of the ramp, he looked around quickly. He must have been satisfied, because he gave a quick wave. All clear. Peter got down off the fishing boat and followed. Elise untied the boat and pulled it around to a safer spot. When Peter made it to the top, he could barely see Henrik at the door of the shack, standing there, kind of bent over. This was going too slowly; he wasn't going in for the oars yet. Peter heard the door rattling. *No! The security guard couldn't have locked the door!*

Henrik turned around where he stood, looking in Peter's direction. He shrugged, making a big wave with his arm. By the time Peter tiptoed up to the shed, Henrik had already slipped up to the little window, pushed it open, and flopped inside.

Good. At least the window was unlocked. Just get in and get out, Henrik, before the guard comes back.

"Come on, Henrik," Peter whispered through a crack. He felt for the padlock on the door, the one his uncle never used. It was locked tightly. But this was taking too long. "Are you in there or what?"

"Yeah," he whispered back. "Oars coming out." Peter scampered up under the window and caught the two oars as Henrik pushed them out. In a second, Henrik was back out beside Peter, and he grabbed one of them under his good arm. Peter looked around carefully for the security guard again, then followed Henrik with his oar, down to the ramp.

This ramp was not a place of good memories, after Henrik's tumble and arm breaking. Henrik stopped for a moment, turned and handed Peter something in the dark. "Here, carry this, would you?" he asked softly. "My hands are full."

The fishing basket didn't feel heavy, but there was something inside that moved a little. "What are we doing with the bird?" Peter whispered as they climbed down the ramp again, this time a little slower, a little more carefully.

"Number One," Henrik explained. "I found out he's Jewish, too, so he has to come along."

14

A Way Through
the Sea

"Here, I'll row first," said Peter as he set up the oars. Elise didn't argue; she just nodded and settled into the stern, the back end, of the boat. She would get her turn in the long row ahead. Actually, Henrik was a much better rower than either of them, when he could use both arms. Peter tended to make a lot more splashes, a lot more noise. Elise was a pretty smooth rower, but not quite as strong. They used to go out rowing more often when they were younger, but lately Elise had stayed home, for her own reasons.

No one said anything about German guards, although all three of them knew the men were probably all around the harbor, watching. At least it was dark, especially when the little moon disappeared behind the clouds. That was happening more and more. Peter looked up as it disappeared again. *I'm not sure how we're going to get out of this one. What happens if we're caught?*

Henrik, who was in the front of the boat, took a deep breath. Peter heard it from his rowing seat.

"Ready?" whispered Henrik.

"I'm ready," said Peter.

Elise had the pigeon basket with her in the back, the stern seat. She put it down for a moment, reached out, and fumbled to pull the boat around a couple of ropes hanging in the water by the dock. They got tangled around the boat, and she glanced about nervously as she worked to get them undone. Elise finally got the lines untangled and pulled her hands back into the boat. "Let's go, Peter," she whispered.

First they had to maneuver around and between the small fishing fleet. It wasn't large because there were quite a few more workboats—big ships and ferries—around this harbor. Always Peter kept the boat in the darkest shadows, behind the boats that were floated together. It was slower going, but he knew all the hiding places. Once, when a light swept the harbor for a moment, he let his oars freeze. They glided past a big black sailing schooner, almost scraping the hull. Then the light was gone, and they crept on.

Peter paused again for a moment, listening to something. He thought he heard voices again. Henrik and Elise turned around and looked, so they must have heard them, too. Then it was quiet again—only the sound of the waves, a little squeak from Peter's rowing, and the ripple of water as they moved through the harbor.

Henrik leaned toward Peter's ear. "Do you believe in angels?" He said it so softly Peter wasn't really sure what he said. Last week, or at least before he went out on that fishing trip with his uncle, Peter might have laughed at the question. Now he wasn't so sure that there might not be some, if he just knew where to look. *If there are any angels in the neighborhood*, thought Peter, pulling quietly on the oars, *we've probably been tripping over them all night.*

From the backseat, Elise was the only one who could see exactly where they were headed. So pretty soon, they developed a pattern: Peter rowed, and Elise steered her brother out of the harbor by tapping either his right or his left ankle with her foot. He would pull more in whichever direction she tapped. Peter could have been blind, and he felt as if he were. *Maybe the guards are blind, too,* thought Peter as he pulled once more. *And deaf. They haven't stopped us . . . yet.*

Peter never could explain how they got out of the harbor without attracting any more attention. But he knew they were past the breakwater when the waves started feeling different. Gradually, he started to get the hang of the rowing, started to get into a stronger, steadier stroke. Pull, rest, recover, pull again. Up one wave swell, then down another.

In the darkness, foam from the waves gurgled by the side of the boat and lit up when the moon peeked from behind the clouds. As Peter got to rowing more steadily, they washed over each wave with a little sideways shimmy. They were going across the Sound, and the waves were coming down the Sound, coming from the darkness, the way all ships came in, from the open ocean. If it had been a calmer night, they might have slipped across without any trouble. But the wind and chop kept hitting them at just the wrong time, pushing the bow of the boat around, sometimes sending salty, icy, stinging spray all over them, and especially all over Henrik. He didn't say a word; he just hung on with one hand, and tucked the other hand underneath his arm, trying to keep warm. Pretty soon, though, he couldn't stop shivering. It was getting windier.

"Can you see the lights?" Peter asked Elise for about the tenth time. Only when they were out on the open water did anyone dare to speak again above a whisper. They had been whispering and hissing all night, it seemed.

"Always," she replied. "You're doing a good job."

A particularly big wave hit the boat just then, jolting the bow up out of the water. Instead of pulling water, there was only air for Peter's right oar. He pulled back hard in the darkness and fell over backwards with a clatter.

"Whoa!" he called, flat on his back in the front of the boat, at Henrik's feet.

Henrik lost his grip and fell over, too, from the rocking of the boat. Elise held on tight to the pigeon basket and managed to stay in her seat.

"Hang on!" yelled Henrik, but no one needed the advice. He was trying to get back up at the same time Peter was, while their little boat was rocking like an out-of-control carousel horse.

Elise was the only one who saw the moonlit pile of foam—about twice as tall as the boat—as it was just about to wash over them. She ducked down, clutching the basket tightly, and closed her eyes. "Peter!" she yelled.

It took everyone a minute to figure out what was happening after the big wave washed through. It didn't so much pound over on top of them, like a wave on a beach does to someone building a sand castle, but it barreled through like a big wet freight train, leaving buckets full of seawater in their little boat. They twirled around two or three times. When Peter looked back out to get his direction, they were pointed straight back at dark Denmark—away from the lights of Sweden.

Elise pulled the pigeon basket out of the ice-cold slosh—it was now around their ankles—and put the poor bird back up on the seat with her. The bird was probably soaked to the feather and as cold as they were. Still, they remained floating, and they had thought ahead.

"Good thing we remembered a bailing bucket," Peter said. Henrik wasn't wasting any time. He was back in his seat, bailing buckets over the side.

"I'll get us dried out in just a couple of minutes," he said. "You saw that we got turned around, right?"

"Yep," replied Peter in a cold whisper. But he didn't say it very loudly at all. He just sat there, not knowing what to do.

"What did you say?" asked Elise.

Henrik looked up for a second from his bailing. "Why don't you start rowing again? We're okay."

Peter still didn't move. "I said yeah, I know we're turned around, and I know we're full of water, and I know we only have one oar."

Henrik stopped bailing, then looked over the side in disgust. Even Elise groaned.

"The oar, though," said Peter, with just a little hope in his voice. "Maybe it's somewhere close by?"

"Can you see it?" Elise said in a tired voice.

Peter looked all around the boat, hoping for a miracle, but he could hardly even tell where they were. *Where are those angels when you need them?* he thought.

It was nowhere. The oar was just gone. So as Henrik continued to pour water over the side, Peter turned around in his seat and tried to paddle the boat like a canoe. It didn't work very well, but he paddled in a circle so at least they were facing the right direction again, toward Sweden. The waves were really bouncing the little boat around now that they were just sitting there.

"How far out do you think we made it?" asked Peter.

Henrik didn't answer, but Elise scanned the water between their boat and the lights. It was hard to tell the distance in the darkness. "Almost halfway, if we're lucky," she guessed.

Peter jammed his oar into the water, disgusted. He wasn't ready to give up, but he was starting to feel tempted. *Yeah, we've been lucky so far. But not now. Not anymore.*

For a while no one said anything. Henrik kept bailing water, dodging out of Peter's way as he struggled with the oar. All of them were feeling sick to their stomachs by that time.

Elise kept the bird basket on her lap, whispering to the homing pigeon. "You're going to be fine," she told the bird. "Just a few more minutes, and we'll be there." She wished she could believe it herself.

"So what would your uncle the sailor do now?" Henrik asked.

Peter paused for a minute. He was out of ideas—really out of ideas—and he knew he wasn't doing too well with just one oar. The waves seemed like they were pushing the boat back to Denmark, farther away from where they wanted to go. But it was hard to tell. He looked around again, trying to figure where they were. *This isn't working*.

"He would pray," said Peter finally. "But he probably would have prayed a long time ago. Maybe that's where we went wrong."

When no one said anything else, Peter went back to his paddling. He tried to remember what his uncle had prayed in the room full of Jewish people. *Something about a way through the water? A way through the sea?* Elise would remember. He didn't want to say anything else, though, so he kept quiet. Somehow, it seemed too long ago, too far away.

"Peter," said Elise. "My turn to row now, okay?"

"You mean paddle, and this is useless," replied Peter. "But I'm still fine. Take over in five minutes."

Finally Peter started to make the boat move just a little, but it was still a zigzag course. Henrik would have done a lot better if he could have used his arms. As it was, all he could do was bail a little water out with his good arm. And the waves—maybe not as big now but still scary—kept pounding the boat, tossing icy spray at them, keeping them soaked and shivering. Peter thought about home for a second. *What a nightmare this is!*

Then he let his thoughts drift back to his uncle and the prayer he couldn't remember. *So why not pray? What could it hurt?* In between paddles, he closed his eyes, trying to remember some good prayer words. His mind was blank, though, so he finally gave up and just started to pray as if he were talking to someone.

As I'm sure you can tell, God, we're looking for some help. This hasn't turned out right—this is awful. Another wave sprayed him straight in the face. Even with his heavy coat, he was already soaked, so he just winced and kept paddling. Maybe they were moving, just a little. *I'm not sure, God, if you're into making deals. But . . .* Peter looked around at the blackness and the waves that didn't stop. Another one hissed by, white foam on the top. *But, God, like I said, we need some help, any kind of help.* That was all he could think of. End of prayer.

"Are you talking to yourself?" asked Henrik from the front of the boat. He was curled up now, after bailing out most of the water.

Peter hadn't realized he was talking out loud. Feeling embarrassed, he tried to play dumb. "Huh, what?"

"You were mumbling," said Henrik. "Talking to yourself."

Peter tried to think of something to say that didn't sound stupid. Instead, he started rambling. "Don't you wish we had a flashlight so we could find the oar?" he said. "I mean, if it were daylight, we'd have no problem seeing it. It's probably just a few feet from us, floating around, but we can't see any farther than we can reach."

"Yeah," agreed Henrik. "Of course, if this little trip was in the daylight, all the Germans would get a pretty good look at us."

Peter kept paddling, wiggling the boat back and forth. Then Elise put her hand out to stop him.

"What's wrong?" he asked.

"I think I hear something," she whispered back. "Do you hear it, Henrik?"

Henrik paused. "Yeah, I hear it," he answered from the front of the boat.

Peter listened, and he thought he could hear it too, in the distance. He wasn't even sure which direction it was coming from, but there it was: a low rumbling sound, far across the water. He thought maybe it was coming from the direction of Denmark, but he wasn't sure. It was slowly getting louder and louder, and it definitely wasn't the *ka-chunk* of a local fishing boat.

"It's getting closer," whispered Elise. They were back to whispers. "Think it's Uncle Morten?"

Peter knew what it was now, and so did the others. He wished it *were* Uncle Morten, but it was the unmistakable, steady hum of a patrol boat. It was still a ways off, though, and the rowboat rocked in the swells. A piece of driftwood bumped into the side of their little boat.

"Hey, would you look at that," Henrik whispered again, this time real low. Peter and Elise could see it, too, almost directly behind them. A red-orange glow, now brighter, now moving just a little bit, kind of like a flag. A cigarette. And it wasn't anyone on Uncle Morten's boat, that was for sure.

"No cigarettes," Uncle Morten had warned the house full of Jews the night before in the Andersen living room. Peter thought back. *Was it just last night? Or last year?*

"When it's dark out there on the water," the fisherman had said, "even the tiny glow of a cigarette acts like a lighthouse for German patrol boats. You think they can't see it, but if it's dark enough, even the Swedes can look out their windows and see you coming."

The German navy patrol didn't seem to realize that it worked both ways, though. Or maybe they didn't care. Either way, the boat was coming their direction. Kind of slow, but coming their direction nonetheless.

The driftwood—Peter thought it must have been an old log—bumped the boat again, right beside where Elise was sitting. She reached down to the water, probably to push it away, but then she startled Peter by grabbing ahold of it instead. Excitedly she pulled the dripping piece of wood up into the boat next to the other oar. "Look what's been banging against the boat for the past five minutes," she whispered in Peter's ear. Now they had two oars again!

Peter's heart jumped—he could hardly believe it! He swiveled around to his old rowing position, mounted the oars in one silent motion, and dug in. This time he didn't head straight to Sweden, but down the Strait. Any direction to get away from the oncoming boat. It was almost on top of them.

The powerful throb of the German boat's engines turned into a steady roar as it got closer and closer. Peter was afraid to look up, thinking his face might shine like a mirror in the dim light. Elise and Henrik hunched down, too. Peter just lowered his head and pulled on the oars until he thought they would snap. He thought he could almost hear Henrik from behind him, cheering him on, only no one was saying anything. Stroke. Stroke. Stroke.

Brighter lights came out of the mist. Peeking up for just a second, Peter could see them in the middle of the boat—glows from sailors' cigarettes on the bridge (the steering room) and from a couple of red lights on the stern. Any second now and they were either going to run the little boat down or snap on their big spotlight. Then that would be it. They could even hear some men laughing over the rumbling sound of the engine.

Thanks for the oar, God, Peter found himself praying again. This time it was a little easier. But there was no more time to think, or to pray. All he could do, one more time, was just keep rowing. He kept rowing, faster and faster, until he thought his lungs would burst and his arms fall off in pain. He thought of nothing else but rowing, pulling the oars, away from the patrol boat with the laughing men, as far as he could go. Each stroke turned into a prayer: *Please, please, please . . .*

It was Henrik who finally shook his shoulders. "They're gone, Peter, they're gone," said Henrik. "Stop rowing for a minute."

At first, it didn't register, and then Elise reached over, stopping his rowing hands. "It's okay, Peter," she echoed Henrik's words. "They're gone."

"How could they not have seen us?" Henrik whispered.

Peter finally understood, and he let the oars glide. *Angels, right?* All he could do was shake in his seat for a minute, then he just slumped down, feeling about as alive as a used dishrag. *I'm the escaping Jew,* thought Peter, *the way I feel. Or I might as well be.*

Then Elise spoke up, with that voice of hers no one messed with. "Here," she said, "it's my turn to row. You've been at it long enough."

Peter didn't argue; he was far past the point of being able to decide much anymore. He and Elise traded seats, and Peter took the bird basket. Henrik stayed where he was, bailing out a little water once in a while. After a few pulls, they picked up their speed again, this time in the right direction. Peter started to catch his breath.

"How long do you figure we've been out now?" he asked, after another half hour.

"Two hours maybe?" Henrik guessed. "No, maybe two and a half. We really ought to be in Swedish waters by now."

At least the lights of Sweden were definitely looking closer. From his position in the back of the boat, he could see them clearly. If it were daytime, he would have been looking for houses, places to row toward, a safe harbor. In the darkness he was looking for a bunch of lights that meant a harbor town, a safe place to land. Any harbor town would do now. Every couple of minutes, as they neared the Swedish coast, they all checked to see.

"I think you're going too far right," said Peter, looking at the lights. "So row a little more to the left, Elise."

"My left?"

"No, the boat's left."

Henrik said he thought they were heading toward a fishing village called Hillarp, a little ways down the coast. The big city of Goteborg was way off to the right, out of reach. The current had pushed them a ways, too.

"I'm almost sure there are a couple of harbors here that we can pull into," said Henrik. He was still bailing out the bottom of the boat. And Number One was still faithfully sitting in the basket. At least, Peter thought he was; no one ever heard a sound from the bird.

As they got closer, Peter's mind wandered again. He thought of his parents, who would surely have returned home by that time to find that Elise and Peter weren't there. In his mind, Peter imagined them reading the note he had scribbled about going down to the harbor. But his parents would know, of course, that they had not made it in time to catch Uncle Morten. *How long will it take for them to find the missing rowboat and figure out what we've done? And how much trouble are we going to be in?* Peter didn't want to think about that part of it. *But what else could we have done? I wish . . .*

Peter's thoughts were interrupted by the sound of another boat, way off in the distance. *Not again!* Elise stiffened at the oars. She stopped rowing, and they all listened. Were their ears playing games now? There was no sound.

Then they all heard it again, the sound of a boat engine. "Which way should I row?" Elise whispered frantically.

"Which way is it coming from?" Henrik whispered back. He swiveled his head around in a circle like an owl, trying to get a fix on the noise.

"I can't tell," said Peter, sniffing the air. "But it *is* getting louder." And closer. In the back of his mind was the question he was afraid to ask. Elise asked it for him. "You don't think they would come this far over, do you?" she asked.

Peter looked at Henrik. They both knew who "they" were. "They" were the ones that had been chasing them all night. "They" were the ones who wanted Henrik's family. "They," thought Peter, were going to give him nightmares for a long time to come.

And now it seemed that "they" were getting closer to the boat, one more time.

"I didn't think they would," whispered Henrik.

Elise still didn't move her oars. "Listen," she said, "that boat is getting awfully close again."

And it was. All they could do this time was duck down into the boat once more, keeping their shiny faces from the light. It didn't do much good, though, because even the little bit of foggy moonlight was enough to light up the boat as they bounced around in the waves. The clouds were mostly gone now. Never mind that the patrol boat had nearly run them down without seeing them. Peter wasn't sure the angels would pull off the same rescue twice.

But he sneaked a peek to see. The dark shape of the boat was almost a soccer field's length away now, but turning away from them in the dark.

"They're going right by us," said Elise into Peter's ear as they crouched down. She had hardly said that when there was a shout from the boat, and it changed course, turning straight for the wave-tossed rowboat.

"That's it," moaned Henrik, and Peter felt himself give up, too. *Henrik's right. It doesn't matter anymore. There's no getting away now.* A searchlight from the boat hit them square in their faces as they tried to see what was going on. The sudden brightness hurt Peter's eyes, and he snapped them shut.

Even though they were finally caught, Peter felt relieved— and a little guilty at the same time. *I'm not supposed to be feeling like this.*

"Can you see anything, Peter?" whispered Elise. Then a man behind the spotlight shouted as the boat pulled up closer.

"Danish? Jews?" boomed the voice, not in the German they had feared, but in a wonderful, musical Swedish. Peter tried to look past the light and saw what looked more like a medium-sized Swedish fishing boat than a German patrol boat.

Henrik stood up and started waving. In his excitement he almost tipped the boat over. Then they all started flapping their arms, as if the Swedes were far away rather than right beside them. The deck above was lined with friendly, rough faces of fishermen.

"Yeah!" Peter and Elise yelled back as loudly as they could. Henrik joined in almost the same breath, so it sounded like a cheer after Peter's soccer team scored a goal. No one would have trouble understanding. "We're Danes!"

"So welcome to Sweden," the man with the searchlight called back.

"We made it, we made it," Henrik repeated as the larger boat nudged alongside. The men in the fishing boat hauled the three of them over the side, then tossed each shivering body a rough wool blanket. They even yanked the wonderful little grayish yellow rowboat up on the deck of their trawler.

Peter wanted to collapse into a corner and sleep, but they had to try and answer questions. Where did they come from? Who were their parents? Why were three kids out there alone? For a minute, they stood on the deck of the fishing boat, looked at one another, and about cried. Peter put his arms around his sister's and Henrik's shoulders. They had made it, but they weren't home yet.

"My parents, Esaias and Ruth Melchior, came over on a fishing boat last night," Henrik said to one of the men in half-Danish, half-Swedish. The man appeared to be the captain, the way he spoke to the others. Besides that, he had a salt-and-pepper beard and stood a head taller than anyone else.

"I'm not sure about your parents," said the man, walking them toward the cabin. "But we can find out soon enough if they made it over tonight." He raised his eyebrow at the three of them. "Lots of people are starting to come across, but what were you doing in that little boat? Shouldn't you have been with your parents?"

They stepped into the warm cabin, where a younger man, maybe not too much older than fourteen, stood behind the wheel. The room was heated by the engine below, a welcome feeling. The noise didn't matter so much.

"It's kind of a long story," Peter offered from under his blanket.

"What's that?" the captain gave him a puzzled look. "A long *book*?"

Wrong word, obviously. They had all taken a couple of years of Swedish in school, but Elise knew the language better than Peter and Henrik. She came to the rescue and said the right thing. The captain smiled. "Your Swedish is fine," he told Peter. "I think between the four of us, we'll get along great." Then he looked at Henrik again. "What was the name of the boat your parents came over in?"

"The *Anna Marie*," Henrik replied. "It was full of people down in the fishhold, I hope."

By now the Swedish captain was making them feel at home in the wheelhouse. They were drinking steaming mugs of something hot, kind of a weak coffee, and they snuggled under the itchy blankets. Already, the nightmarish row was fading into the past, where all of them wanted it to fade, and fast. The blankets, even though they smelled like a combination of fish oil, cigar smoke, and diesel fuel, were great. They were just starting to warm up when Captain Knut (they never learned his last name) gently brought his boat home to a pier. It was dark, and Peter had no idea where they were.

The captain leaned out of the wheelhouse, letting in the cold, early morning air. He called out a couple of commands in Swedish, too fast for even Elise to understand, and the deckhands jumped off each end of the boat, rope in hand. He shut off the engine, and everything fell quiet again. Peter felt a big hand on his shoulder.

"Well," said the captain, "you're a little light, but still a fine catch for a night's work." He winked at Peter, but Peter could barely make out the man's face in the dim light of the wheel-house. "I think my crew and I are going to be fishers of men and women and kids until you're all safely over here. We've lost count how many we've seen already. But now, you have to tell me a little about yourselves. You're related?"

Henrik looked at Peter and Elise with his famous grin. It was coming back.

"Yeah," he said, "kind of. But we do have different parents. Theirs are back in Denmark, and mine are . . ." His voice trailed off, and Elise finished the sentence for him.

"His are the ones we told you about, the ones that were sup-posed to have come over on the *Anna Marie*. It's my uncle's boat. Henrik here was supposed to have been on the boat, too."

Henrik, Elise, and Peter took turns from there telling the story—about all the running, the security guard, the drunk sol-dier at the pub, the idea to row across, the patrol boat. The cap-tain listened thoughtfully, nodding his head and stroking his beard. Once in a while, he asked another question.

"And we thought your boat maybe was a German patrol boat, chasing us all the way over, or coming back or something," finished Henrik. "I guess you know what happened after that."

"Sounds more like a bad dream than real life," said the cap-tain. "If I hadn't picked you up myself out of the water, I might not have believed it."

"But you really haven't heard of the *Anna Marie*?" Henrik asked one more time. "My parents?"

"Like I said," the captain repeated politely. "If they made it to somewhere close, we'll be sure to find them as soon as we can."

If, thought Peter. Right now that was the most terrible word in the dictionary, Danish or Swedish. "If" they made it.

"What do you mean, 'If they made it'?" Henrik asked, fiddling with a spoke on the fishing boat's large wooden steering wheel.

"I just mean," the man looked down, "not every single boat crossing over from Denmark is going to make it over here, I'm sorry to say. Most are, though. You kids probably did a lot of growing up in a very short time out there, and you know all about the German patrols, from your story."

They knew.

"But I can promise you this," said the fisherman, his voice brightening. "I can help you find them tomorrow morning." He looked at a little clock next to the steering wheel. One A.M. "I mean, later this morning. If they're to be found, we'll steer you in the right direction before I go out again fishing for real fish."

Peter was pretty sure that's what he said. His eyes were closed by then, and he was trying hard to listen, but he fell asleep standing up, leaning against the side of the boat. Captain Knut noticed him, smiled, and patted his shoulder.

"And you, little Dane, we're going to have to get you and your sister back to Helsingor before your parents go absolutely crazy with worry."

"They already have, I'm sure," said Peter, feeling more weary than he had ever felt in his life.

"Well, you surely can't row back."

No argument there.

"If our uncle is still around . . ." Elise volunteered. She, too, was barely holding on, about to fall asleep.

"We will see tomorrow. Tomorrow," finished the captain. "But right now, it's already morning." He had never explained to them what he was doing out at that time of night, but everyone was too tired to ask now. "You kids will sleep here on the boat."

Again no argument. The man steered them toward a little room behind the wheelhouse with two narrow bunks on each side, one above the other. He shoved a pile of dry clothes into Henrik's arms.

"There should be something that will fit you in there," said Captain Knut. Then he was gone. Peter and Henrik gratefully crashed into a cocoon of blankets and cushions. Elise found a bunk in the empty pilothouse, and she was asleep in a minute.

In his little bunk above Peter, Henrik was tossing about, trying to get comfortable.

"Hey, Henrik," Peter broke the silence. "Are you awake?"

"Where have I heard that question before?" he asked. "No, I'm asleep. I feel like sleeping for a year. I was asleep fifteen minutes ago."

Peter felt just as tired, but he had to say something. *Maybe I won't see him again for a long time.* "Henrik, do you think you'll come back soon?"

"I don't know, Peter," he said, sounding farther away. "All I can think about is finding my mom and dad."

"I know." There was a pause. "I'll take care of Number One for you."

Then it was quiet, and Peter thought his friend had fallen asleep.

"Thanks, Peter. Thanks for everything."

"It was nothing."

"Liar. It was too something."

Peter smiled but couldn't say anything else. The last thing he remembered was Henrik kind of moaning as he dropped off to sleep. It sounded as if he were saying something, or calling out, but Peter was too tired to understand anyway. He let his hand flop down to the pigeon's basket. Someone had stashed it there on the floor between the two bunks. He gently poked his finger at the bird, which rustled a little at his touch. *We'll check on Number One in the morning.* It had been a long trip for a bird in a basket.

On the Other Side

Peter thought it had to be a dream, the way voices were yelling all around him. He was wrapped up in old blankets, wearing someone else's old work clothes, and his bed was rocking. *Probably Elise, trying to get me up*. But it was men yelling, and they were all yelling in a language he couldn't understand, at least not completely.

Then his head started to clear. *No dream. This is Sweden*. Henrik was snoring in the bunk above him. Elise was on the boat, too, and they were in the little cabin of Captain Knut's fishing boat. The voices outside were fishermen and dock workers, yelling the same kinds of things in Swedish Peter heard all his life on the docks back home in Helsingor. He popped up on one elbow to see what was going on and knocked his head silly on the bunk bed frame above his head. That was a sure way to wake up in a hurry.

"Hey," mumbled Henrik from somewhere under his blankets. "What's going on?"

Peter didn't say anything, but he felt the boat rock slightly as someone got on. It seemed as though he had just fallen asleep, and he had, really—five hours earlier. In a moment, the man from the night before, Captain Knut, poked his head into the tiny cabin. It wasn't completely light out yet, but there was a little bit of pink morning sunshine showing through a small porthole.

"The sun is rising in the east!" rumbled the man in a kind of bass voice that shook the last sleep from everyone's head. He was singing a Danish song, but it sounded like something only halfway between the two languages, close as they were.

Okay, okay, we're awake. Both boys groaned.

"Hey, come on," said the captain. "Your sister is already up. And I thought you wanted to find your parents."

"That's Henrik," replied Peter, his eyes still closed. "I just wanted to catch a ride back home on my uncle's boat."

"Right." The big fisherman nodded. "I've made a couple of calls already this morning, and I've found out where most of the Danish people went to last night. Mostly to the big city."

"Hälsingborg," said Elise. She was wide awake and had popped her head into the little cabin. Peter didn't feel alive—yet.

"Right again. Mostly your Danish boats have been coming over just into our waters, and then the people—I mean the Jews—are transferred over to Swedish boats. It works better that way. The Danish boats are free to return quickly, and they don't attract as much attention that way."

He looked around as if to see if anyone was listening. Elise pulled on her brother's foot. "Hey—are you awake, Peter?" she asked.

Peter didn't answer, so Captain Knut looked at Elise. "But not always," he continued. "I also found out that two or three boats came all the way over, to the harbor just up the coast at Viken, the—"

"Which ones?" Henrik and Peter interrupted at the same time. They were awake now.

"I was just telling you," he laughed. "The *Saint Hans* and the *Anna Marie*. Either of those sound familiar?"

He already knew, of course. Henrik had told him all about the boat the night before. The *Anna Marie*!

Within five minutes, they had piled into someone's rusty Volvo car. Henrik, Elise, Peter, and the bird took the backseat; Captain Knut and another fisherman he introduced as Gunnar sat in the front. They munched on crusty bread and cheese from the boat, and Henrik tried to feed the bird. Elise looked over at the boys and laughed.

"What's so funny?" asked Peter, giving her a puzzled look. He was wearing a pair of paint-spattered work pants, and a sweater that had been used as a rag, probably in the engine room.

"Your clothes," she said. "You look like you just washed up on the beach."

"As a matter of fact"—Peter tried to act serious—"I did, and so did you. And you don't look too great either."

Elise had to wear a ripped old pair of dark green slacks and a red sweater; both were way too big for her. They all looked funny, but who could complain? They were warm, dry, and starting to feel fed again. The captain chattered in the front as they bumped down the Swedish country road. Henrik kept feeding bread to his hungry bird.

"They're in the next town up the coast, like I said." Peter saw the captain's eyes in the rearview mirror as he spoke. "That's all I could find out, except that there was some kind of problem with one of the boats. Probably that's why they came all the way over. Engine trouble or something."

"You're not sure?" Henrik asked, a worried expression on his face.

"They didn't say. They didn't know."

Their new friend never said who "they" were; but no one asked. Peter remembered the other "they" from the night before and shuddered. He was glad just to be there.

"It's just down the road here," said Captain Knut after a few more minutes. His crew member didn't say anything, only grinned and nodded once in a while. He wasn't following this mixture of Swedo-Danish.

The captain was right; it wasn't five minutes before they pulled out of the coastal woods, down a small hill into a clearing, and then into the middle of the harbor town: Viken. It was clustered around a small, rocky bay, where a few tired-looking fishing boats sat at anchor. More workboats were tied up at what looked like the town's main pier. Henrik strained out the window for a look, and the car came lurching around the last corner before the waterfront.

Peter caught sight of the *Anna Marie*'s bright blue trim first. "I see it!" he whooped.

"Where? Really?" Henrik missed it, then it was right in front of the car as they skidded in the gravel yard by the pier.

"Here we are," said the captain. Henrik and Peter were flying out the doors even before the car was all the way stopped.

A couple of fishermen were down by the pier already; one of them almost dropped his toolbox as the three crazy Danish kids sprinted down to the *Anna*. The little fishing boat was tied up at the pier, between two Swedish boats about the same size.

Captain Knut asked the men on the waterfront a few quick questions, and they pointed to a cluster of brightly painted yellow and white houses on a street that tumbled straight down from the low hills behind the harbor. A couple of people were walking down the narrow street, out for their morning chores. Peter wondered where everyone could be, but not for long.

"Henrik! Henrik Melchior! You stay right there!" a man bellowed in Danish. They couldn't tell where the shout came from, so they just stood there, looking bewildered. There was a stirring in one of the houses, and people started to run around inside. A window slammed, then a door, and then two people were racing down the street. It was Henrik's parents, moving faster than Peter had ever seen them move before.

"Henrik! Henrik! Henrik!" His mom was sobbing before she even reached the pier, and then there was a tangle of hugging and kissing, and more hugging. This went on for what seemed forever to Peter. He and Elise got dragged into it a couple of times, even though he tried to stay out. He came up for air and saw the captain leave for his car. Knut looked straight at Peter and Henrik.

"Thanks," Peter shouted at him. By now he couldn't help crying too, like Elise and the rest.

"Thousand thanks," Henrik added, waving at the man.

Captain Knut just smiled a broad smile, nodded for a moment, and ducked into the little car with his crewman. In a moment, they had disappeared down the road, leaving behind only a blue cloud of smoke. Then Mr. Melchior held Peter and Elise by the shoulders and shook them in a friendly way.

"So you're the ones responsible for bringing my son to safety, are you?" His face was streaming with tears. Peter hadn't known dads could cry like that, too.

"We just couldn't think of what else to do, sir," Peter explained. "You see, we were watching what happened out on the street, and Henrik got left behind, and he was supposed to be in the trunk of the last car, but then he had to go to the bathroom, and—"

"That's okay," Mr. Melchior interrupted Peter's stammering. "There's plenty of time now to tell the story. What matters most is that we are safe—and together." Mrs. Melchior tugged on his arm. "And you'll have much to talk about with your father here, Peter and Elise."

"My father?" said Elise, not understanding. "Here? What about Uncle Morten?"

"He will best explain that to you," said Mr. Melchior, suddenly very serious. "We've had a long trip, too, I'm afraid, in more ways than one. And a costly one."

That's when Peter felt another hand on his shoulder, and he turned around to look straight up at his own father. *Dad! What is he doing here?*

Elise saw her father at the same time, and she launched herself up, arms around his neck, the way she used to when she was a little girl.

The twins nearly squeezed the breath out of their father, and it wasn't until they were back in the warm living room of the local inn that it started to sink in for Peter: *Dad is really here, here in Sweden. Dad the stranger, the one who never knew what was going on. Dad the rescuer.*

Mr. Andersen hardly said a word as Elise and Peter spilled out the whole story, for the second time, from the mixup with the escape car to the long, long ride in the little rowboat. Peter told him everything, even a few things he hadn't told Captain Knut, like the times he got seasick and how scared he was. Elise told him about almost getting caught in the streets of Helsingor and how they had run. It didn't seem to matter now what kind of trouble they might get into; they just told him everything.

Mr. Andersen nodded, listening carefully to every word. His two children must have gone on for something like an hour, nonstop. But finally they were done, and to Peter it was as if he had just unloaded the biggest burden he had ever carried.

Then Mr. Andersen scooted his chair up closer, and he looked straight at both of them. "Elise, Peter, I'm proud of you," he said quietly. It was their turn to listen. "Even though as your father it scares me to death to hear what you did."

"Because you did the same thing?" asked Peter.

"Maybe, Peter. The important thing—and I think Henrik's father said this already—is that you're both safe. And because of what you did, the Melchiors are all safe."

Then a dark thought flashed across Peter's mind. "But what about Uncle Morten?" he asked. "You haven't told me what happened to him, or even why you're here."

Elise looked at her father with a worried expression.

Peter's father pressed his lips together, stood up, and looked out of the room's small window. No one had been in or out since they had been sitting there, only an old woman Peter assumed was the innkeeper.

"You know, I always admired my brother," said Mr. Andersen to the window. The sun was streaming in on his face. "He was always the brave one. But we were so different. He took after your grandfather—fishing . . . the outdoors. He could do everything."

Peter wasn't sure if that was the answer yet to his question, so he kept still. Elise sat there, too, knotting her fingers.

"I was the studious one," he continued. "The clever one, the one who could figure. A lot like you, Peter. And in some ways, like you, too, Elise. So I ended up in the bank—counting." He looked down at his hands. They were scratched and bruised. Peter's and Elise's hands weren't very pretty either, with all the blisters. They hurt like fire now that Peter thought of them. Elise's hair was tangled like spaghetti, too, but somehow none of that mattered.

"It's not that I regret it, it's just . . ." He turned around and faced Peter and Elise. His eyes were brimming with tears now, and Peter still didn't know what had happened to Uncle Morten. "Your uncle was captured on the beach last night," he said finally. His voice cracked. "We had everyone loaded on the boat except Mr. Lumby and the people who were supposed to come in the Mercedes. We didn't know what had happened to them, but we couldn't wait any longer. Morten decided to take one last look for them, and he took the rowboat back to the beach. A German patrol—they had a dog—came down the beach just then. Morten didn't have a chance to run or anything. There was just no chance."

"But what did you do, Dad?" Peter said, stunned.

"We couldn't do anything, except head out of there as fast as we could. We had to take a zigzag, roundabout course. I'm still not sure why no one caught us before we reached Sweden. We kept going all the way over, and the engine was making a funny noise. I'm surprised we didn't run you kids over out there rowing around."

"But what will happen to Uncle Morten now?" asked Elise.

"I don't know, Elise. First he'll probably stay in a prison somewhere in Denmark. Maybe Vestre Prison, in Copenhagen. They'll try to force information out of him. But I doubt if the Germans will learn much from him."

Peter squirmed in his chair at the thought of his uncle in a prison, a prison with Nazi guards. "Is there any chance he'll get out, Dad?"

"I don't know. I just can't tell you, because I don't know."

Then Elise jumped up suddenly. "Mom!" she cried. "Where was Mom during all this?"

"That's the other thing," explained Mr. Andersen. "Apparently all sorts of things happened after I left with the first car. I was surprised—and upset—to find your mother in the second car, riding with old Mrs. Clemmensen. But we got them untangled, and Mrs. Clemmensen finally got in the boat somehow. I told your mom to wait in the truck, to wait for me so we could drive back home together."

"But you never got back to the car!" said Elise, horrified.

"She would have figured it out, I know," he said. But even he looked a bit worried. "She's going to be out of her mind at home, though, even if she is all right. I'll tell you this." He looked at Elise and pointed down for emphasis. "I'm going to make sure she never has to go through this kind of thing again. And you, too."

That was all they talked about the rest of the day: Mom, how worried she would be, and getting home as soon as they could. They had to wait until it was dark again, a terribly long time. Then there was a second goodbye with the Melchiors, who would stay in Sweden for the rest of the war, however much longer it lasted. Peter's father had to leave the *Anna Marie* over in Sweden, too, and Mr. Melchior was left in charge of finding a place for it, someone who could care for it for a few months. It was no use, said Mr. Andersen, taking it right back to Denmark.

"How could we explain coming back in that boat," he asked, "especially if the Nazis figured out who it belonged to?"

When night fell again, the three Andersens ended up getting a ride back over in a Swedish boat, one of the boats tied up right next to the *Anna Marie*. As they retraced their route back toward home, Peter sat in the corner of the dark wheelhouse, staring out the window. Elise was quiet, too, until one of the three Swedish fishermen on the boat came up to speak to the man steering. They spoke for a moment in low tones, pulled a chart from a rack overhead, and briefly turned a flashlight on to study it. Peter and Elise both stared at the man's face, lit up for a moment in the light. Peter started to sputter.

"You're the man in the woods!" Peter was finally able to say, above the clatter of the boat engine.

"You've met this man before?" asked Mr. Andersen.

"A few months ago," explained Elise. "In the woods. By accident, and he was with Uncle Morten."

Finally the Swedish man remembered, and he smiled slightly.

"Oh, yes, you must be Morten's niece and nephew," said the man, looking up from his chart, "the ones who came crashing through the woods that day." Then his expression clouded over. "I heard what happened to your uncle, your brother. I'm sorry." He turned away from Peter and Elise, and looked back out the window toward the darkness of Sweden. Then he stepped out of the wheelhouse, leaving them alone again.

"Do you remember what Uncle Morten called him?" Peter asked his sister.

"Olaf, I think," she answered. Neither of them said anything else for a time.

Mr. Andersen didn't ask how they had met Olaf, but after a while he looked at his two quiet children again. Both of them were staring out the window at the dark waves. "Aren't you tired?" he asked them.

"Not really," answered Peter. Somehow he wasn't. Or if his body was tired, his mind wouldn't let go. Too many pictures were flashing through. The escape. The row over. The soldiers. The running. His mom. Captain Knut's rescue. His father in Sweden. The story about Uncle Morten. And now seeing Olaf. Everything jumbled together, and Peter couldn't tell where one picture started and the other ended. He thought about things he wished he had done, and still wanted to do, and he thought of what his uncle had told him about being a Christian. And then he had seen a new side of his dad, a dad he had missed before.

Henrik? It was as if Peter and Elise had lost a friend, but not really. There would be another time, after the war, Peter hoped, when Henrik and his family would come back. *I could even take care of their place until then. Or someone could rent it.* Lots of other Danes would do the same for the Jewish Danes they knew. It was just what friends did.

He looked over at his sister. In the darkness he could make out her face but not much else. She had her nose pressed against the glass, looking out, probably thinking some of the same things.

They made it back to Denmark an hour later and found a dark beach, close to the same beach where Uncle Morten was captured. With the boat's engine shut off, Olaf quietly pulled the line of a small boat they had dragged behind them, like a dog on a leash. He motioned with his hand and barely whispered. "In you go," he said. "You're almost home."

Without a word, the four of them stepped carefully into the little boat. Peter and Elise perched in the back end, Mr. Andersen in the front, Olaf in the middle. They slipped away from the larger fishing boat, and Olaf rowed quietly up to within a few yards of the shore.

As they were about to get out of the little boat, Mr. Andersen tried to thank the Swede, but he just shook his head.

"No, you don't thank me," said the Swede. "Your brother would have done the same thing for me."

So without another word, Mr. Andersen helped Elise and Peter slip over the side, and waded the last few steps through icy water to home. Olaf nodded at Elise and Peter, pulled hard on his oars, and shot back to his boat.

This time, Peter was glad there was no one to meet them. Cold, tired, and wet, they hiked back through the woods, found a thickly covered place, and dozed until the morning light gave them permission to hike the last few miles home. Peter's Swedish shoes never dried, and they made squishy noises all the way.

"You know what, kids?" Mr. Andersen finally broke the silence as they turned onto a busier street. He was in between Elise and Peter, and he had his arms around both their shoulders. Morning traffic was starting to stir around the old city, and they could see the buildings of the old section of town. Elise just looked up at him sleepily. Then he reached around and mussed her hair, the way he used to do when she was little. She smiled weakly. "Your mom is going to need a day's worth of hugs when we get home."

She did. It was even more emotional when they walked back into their apartment than it had been in Sweden. The hugs, the kisses. In between more hugs, Mrs. Andersen explained how she had sneaked through the bushes the night before to find everyone on the beach gone. Everyone, fortunately, including the German patrol. The only thing for her to do had been to drive carefully home and wait. Grandfather had stayed there with her.

When Grandfather heard the whole story, though, he was hit hard by the news about Uncle Morten. For over an hour, he just sat completely still in Peter's favorite stuffed chair in their living room, staring straight ahead. Mr. Andersen, who had explained everything to him, came over and put his hand on his father's shoulder.

"Dad, believe me. There was nothing we could do."

Grandfather's eyes flashed with anger, but not at his son. "Maybe not, Arne, but I should have been there." He let out his breath. "And I wasn't." Then he got up and started to pace around the apartment.

"Maybe we can find a way to get him out," suggested Peter as his grandfather brushed by. Peter looked around, making sure no one else heard them. "Maybe if we prayed, something would happen, Grandpa. I . . . I prayed when we were running away with Henrik."

His grandfather stopped and stared at Peter. He looked like he was surprised to hear his grandson talk about prayer. Then a smile spread over his face, and he nodded. He took Peter by the arm as they walked into the hallway.

"Yes, maybe something would happen," he said. "So let's be sure to do that. But how—"

Elise came down the hall just then, looking for Peter and her grandfather. "Grandfather? Have you been down to the boat-house?" she asked. "Henrik may have let his pigeon go by now."

"The pigeon," said her grandfather. "Oh, yes." He gave Peter a wink, his way of telling him that he would not forget what they had started to talk about. "I mean, no, I haven't been down there today, but you two could run down and check."

Peter and Elise didn't need any more encouragement. They raced all the way down to the boathouse.

"Maybe Number One is waiting already," said Elise as they pushed open the boathouse door.

Actually, the bird wasn't really waiting, but he was doing his daily strutting routine, bobbing his head, marching in place, and generally making a lot of noise. Elise cornered him inside the cage.

"Come on, give me the message," said Peter as he unclipped the capsule. The bird didn't struggle much, only pedaled his legs a little, like a bird on a bicycle. Peter had to smile. The homing pigeon seemed to know he was carrying something important, after all that time in the basket. "Thanks, Number One," Peter told the bird as Elise gently tossed him back to the others, to his water dish and to his food.

Nervously, Peter unscrewed the halves of the tiny capsule and hurried to pull out the scrap of paper. It was wrinkled, the back of a candy wrapper. Henrik had obviously worked hard to write in small, neat letters on it. Peter squinted and moved over to the sunlight coming in through the tiny window.

"Let me see," said Elise, and she crowded over to take a look.

"Safe in Sweden," Peter read aloud. "Thanks to you both. Please take care of Number One until I get back. Your friend always, Henrik."

Below that, Henrik had added something else. *A Bible verse?* thought Peter. *This was really from Henrik?* Peter looked closer. It was his friend's handwriting, for sure.

"There's something else," he said.

Elise took the note; it was her turn to read aloud. "Isaiah forty-three," she said, looking up at Peter. "From the Bible?"

"Of course it's from the Bible," said Peter, just as puzzled as his sister. "Read it."

"Isaiah forty-three. 'This is what the Lord says, he who made a way through the sea, a path through the mighty waters . . .' "

Then she looked up, and they both knew what Henrik had meant. About the way through the sea, and about who had made it for them. Without a word, she handed the candy wrapper back over to Peter, who stuffed it into his pants pocket. Closing the door of the shed behind them, they walked down the street toward home. But Peter had one more thing he had to do.

"You go ahead, Elise," he told his sister. "I have to do something."

"Sure," she replied and headed in the direction of home.

"Oh, hey, Elise, I forgot to tell you."

"Yeah?" She looked back, and Peter realized then that they had changed a lot over the last few days. Even though they had their little fights, he and his sister had always gotten along pretty well. But now there was something extra, and they both knew it.

"I forgot to tell you thanks for sticking up for me, when Keld and Jesper were after me the other day."

"No problem," she said easily, with a little smile. "See you at home." She turned and trotted off down the street, leaving Peter by the pier.

"Thanks," he said again, under his breath. Peter looked out at the boats and the place where the *Anna Marie* used to tie up. He had saved a corner of the crusty bread roll Captain Knut had given them back in Sweden. He pulled it out of his coat pocket, crushed it in his hand, and tossed the crumbs as hard as he could out into the harbor.

EPILOGUE

There are many true stories of the rescue of Danish Jews during World War II, even though this one uses fictional characters. In the space of just a few days, thousands of men, women, and children were hidden in Danish homes, and the Danish people helped them to escape. The rescue of the Jews was a bright spot in the dark year of 1943; out of about seven thousand Danish Jews, only a few hundred were captured. It made the German leader, Hitler, furious.

Part of the reason so many escaped from Denmark was because everyone agreed that they would not let their friends and neighbors be captured and sent to prison or death. That had already happened in other parts of Europe. All at once, everyone in the country knew what they had to do. They weren't afraid to do the right thing, no matter what the risk.

Just like Moses. One writer has said that if the Danish rescue of the Jews had happened during Bible times, it would have been included as another chapter in the Old Testament. Who knows? The story does remind us of the Exodus account, when God's people escaped through the Red Sea. God was working in special ways then, and again in 1943.